Praise for David Lubar's Weenies Stories

"This collection will be interesting to middle-grade readers, both reluctant and voracious, who are looking for scary stories and are not easily grossed out."

—*School Library Journal* on *Wipeout of the Wireless Weenies*

"Whoever thinks the short story is dead, or that kids don't like short stories, hasn't talked to any real live kids and hasn't read the latest in this popular series."

—*School Library Journal* on *Attack of the Vampire Weenies*

"This book will talk itself right off the shelves, and reluctant readers will devour it."

—*School Library Journal* on *The Curse of the Campfire Weenies*

"Girls and boys alike will be drawn to Lubar's chilling tales and wicked sense of humor. . . . Perfect for setting the mood at slumber parties and spooky campfires, these tales are the next generation of ghost stories and urban legends."

—*San Francisco Book Review* on *Attack of the Vampire Weenies*

"With supernatural events and creatures, the short and supershort stories are fun, fast-paced reading for Weenies fans and new readers."

—*Booklist* on *Beware the Ninja Weenies*

BOOKS BY DAVID LUBAR

Story Collections

Attack of the Vampire Weenies and Other Warped and Creepy Tales

The Battle of the Red Hot Pepper Weenies and Other Warped and Creepy Tales

Beware the Ninja Weenies and Other Warped and Creepy Tales

The Curse of the Campfire Weenies and Other Warped and Creepy Tales

In the Land of the Lawn Weenies and Other Warped and Creepy Tales

Invasion of the Road Weenies and Other Warped and Creepy Tales

Wipeout of the Wireless Weenies and Other Warped and Creepy Tales

Extremities: Stories of Death, Murder, and Revenge

Novels

Flip

Hidden Talents

True Talents

Character, Driven (forthcoming)

Monsterrific Tales

Hyde and Shriek

The Vanishing Vampire

The Unwilling Witch

The Wavering Werewolf

The Gloomy Ghost

The Bully Bug

Nathan Abercrombie, Accidental Zombie Series

My Rotten Life

Dead Guy Spy

Goop Soup

The Big Stink

Enter the Zombie

WIPEOUT OF THE WIRELESS WEENIES

AND OTHER WARPED AND CREEPY TALES

DAVID LUBAR

A TOM DOHERTY ASSOCIATES BOOK
NEW YORK

This is a work of fiction. All of the characters, organizations, and events portrayed in these stories are either products of the author's imagination or are used fictitiously.

WIPEOUT OF THE WIRELESS WEENIES AND OTHER WARPED AND CREEPY TALES

A Starscape Book
Published by Tom Doherty Associates, LLC
175 Fifth Avenue
New York, NY 10010

www.tor-forge.com

ISBN 978-0-7653-8189-7

Printed in the United States of America

S 0 9 8 7 6 5 4 3 2 1

For Doug Baldwin, Connie Cook, Fern, Heather, and Sylvia—
priceless friends who have done so much
to help make these stories possible

CONTENTS

WIPEOUT OF THE WIRELESS WEENIES

AND OTHER WARPED AND CREEPY TALES

AFTER THE APOCALYPSE

"Zombies!" Dad screamed, pointing out the living room window.

"Where?" Fear and curiosity fought a short battle in my brain. Curiosity won. I rushed over to see for myself.

"No! It's too gruesome," Dad said as he snatched me off my feet, tossed me over his shoulder, and ran toward the basement door. I'm almost twelve, but I'm pretty skinny.

Mom grabbed my twin brother, Eli, and hurried down the stairs right behind us. Eli's also skinny, and Mom's pretty strong.

"Into the shelter," Dad said. "You know the drill."

We sure did. Mom and Dad had us practice our Zombie Apocalypse drill once a week. Whatever we were doing, when Dad screamed, "Zombies!" we had to drop everything and run to the shelter.

"I guess it's not a drill this time," Eli said as Dad bolted the steel door that would keep us safe from the throngs of walking dead.

"Guess not. They never do two drills in one week, and we

had one three days ago. This must be the real thing." I sighed and sat on the couch. The shelter was comfortable enough. There was plenty of food, and a small toilet in a separate room. We had beds and chairs. But it was kind of boring. I like to go outside and play with my friends. Especially now that school was out for the summer. And I had a birthday coming up in less than a week. So did Eli, of course, since we're twins. A zombie apocalypse would ruin everything.

Dad turned on the radio, but all we got was static. It looked like we wouldn't be able to find out what was happening. I grabbed a book and settled down. When I got tired of reading, I unfolded my cot and went to sleep.

The next morning, after breakfast, Dad said, "I'm going to go take a look outside." He grabbed an ax from its peg on the wall and headed for the door.

"Be careful," Mom said. She unbolted the door, then locked everything up again as soon as Dad stepped out. She waited right there with her hand on the bolt, ready to let him back in as soon as he shouted the password.

Dad was only gone for about ten minutes. When he came back in, pounded on the door, and shouted, "Off with their heads!" He was panting, like he'd been running. I spotted something splattered across his shirt. It looked like brains, though I didn't really want to get close enough to it to find out for sure. I noticed the head of the ax was coated with slimy clots, too.

"Is it bad out there?" Mom asked.

"It's not good. We'd better stay here until things calm down," Dad said. "According to everything I've read, they'll start to fall apart eventually. They're rotting. We just have to wait them out."

He checked outside every morning. Each time, he was gone a bit longer. I lost track of the date. But at some point, Mom pulled a cake from the freezer and stuck candles in it.

"Happy Birthday, boys! I put this here just in case," she said. She pulled a small pile of presents from under her bed.

So Eli and I celebrated our birthday in our zombie shelter.

The next day, after Dad went out to check, he came back, hung the ax on its peg, and said, "Good news. It's over."

"They're all gone?" Mom asked.

"All gone," Dad said. "And the government troops removed the bodies."

"Yay! We can go outside!" I shouted. I raced for the door.

"Wait!" Dad grabbed me and Eli by the shoulder. "Remember, this was a terrible experience for all of the survivors. If you see the neighbors, they might not want to talk about it. Okay?"

"Sure." I threw the bolt and flung open the door.

Eli followed me through the house and out to the front yard.

"I hope none of our friends got killed," I said.

"They didn't," he said.

"How do you know?"

"Think about it," he said.

"Think about what?"

"Remember when we turned eight?" he asked.

"Sure. We had that huge party, with the magician and the ice cream cones. It was awesome." I could still taste the hot fudge. I even licked some of it off the couch after it got spilled there.

"Right—it was awesome. But it was kind of a mess, too." Eli said. "And remember when we turned nine?"

"Yeah. Dad took a bunch of us bowling." That was definitely

memorable. Dad threw his back out. And my friends got so rowdy, we were banned from the bowling alley for life. Then, Eli threw up in the car. I guess he shouldn't have eaten five hot dogs. Neither should I. But at least I didn't puke until I got back home. I glanced at the couch. The puke stain wasn't nearly as bad as the fudge stain.

"What about when we turned ten?" Eli asked.

"We didn't have a party. Remember? There was an alien invasion." As the words left my mouth, I realized how crazy they sounded. *Alien invasion*. Almost as crazy as last year, when we'd missed our party because of the killer solar flare. Both times, Dad had suggested the neighbors wouldn't want to relive the experiences, so we never talked about it.

"Eli," I said.

"What?"

"There aren't any zombies, are there?"

"I'm pretty sure that's the case," he said.

I thought about the cake. It was hard to believe Mom had just happened to think of putting one down there, in case the zombie apocalypse overlapped our birthday. There'd been a cake, and presents, down there last year, and the year before, too. "So our parents would rather hide in the basement for a week than throw another birthday party for us?"

"It seems that way."

"What about that stuff on the ax?" I asked.

"Blueberry pudding," Eli said. "I tasted it."

I thought about all of that—alien invasion, solar flare, zombie apocalypse. . . . "What do you think it will be next year?"

"I don't know," he said. "But I do know one thing. We need to get a video game system down there before then."

"Yeah, but no zombie games," I said. "I've definitely had enough zombies for a while."

I grabbed our basketball and headed toward the playground with Eli. As I walked down the street in the fresh air and sunshine, I realized that the one thing I'd never liked about being a twin actually turned out to be an advantage.

"It could be worse," I said.

"What do you mean?" Eli asked.

"Imagine what would happen if we didn't share a birthday," I said. "We'd get stuck in the shelter twice a year."

I threw him a bounce pass and promised myself that if I ever had kids, they could have as many parties as they wanted, no matter how messy things got.

DEAD MEAT

The place smelled like sawdust and blood. But in a good way. Beneath those smells lurked subtler scents of aged salami and smoked sausages. Tyler liked the mingled aromas. He liked the slippery feel of sawdust on the wooden floor. And he liked the way the meat tasted when his mom cooked it. But he didn't like the butcher.

The man was big, as if all the years he'd spent wrestling slabs of beef and large sections of pork had shaped him in the image of his offerings. He was loud, too—shouting at his assistants if they moved too slowly, and even yelling at customers if they dawdled while placing their orders. But this was the only butcher shop in town, and his meat was much better than what was offered in either of the two local supermarkets. So people put up with his anger and his tantrums.

Normally, Tyler entered the butcher shop only when he was running errands with his mother. Until now, he'd never had to face the man alone. Today, he was on his own. His mother wanted to bake a peach pie for a neighbor who'd been restricted to bed while she recovered from surgery. So Tyler was given the shopping list and instructions not to anger Mr. Schmatzler.

No way I'm doing that, Tyler thought as he approached the store. *I'm in and out.*

The brick single-story building was squeezed between a shoe-repair shop, which had its own rich aromas of leather and polish, and a bank, which smelled of nothing. A hand-scrawled sign in the window of the butcher shop advertised lamb shanks and kielbasa.

Tyler rubbed his thumb and fingers against the folded bills in his left front pocket. He shifted his hand and touched the list his mother had given him. Then he reached out and put his fingers on the door handle.

In and out.

He pulled the door open. A shout greeted him.

"I don't need your business!" Mr. Schmatzler yelled as a woman escaped through the doorway, nearly knocking Tyler over.

"Don't ask for a pound when you want half a pound!" the butcher screamed at her fleeing back. "I can't unslice it!"

Tyler recovered his balance, briefly considered heading home and telling his mom the shop was closed, realized he was a terrible liar, sighed twice, then made his way inside. He felt as if the butcher's scream had the ability to push against him like a fierce, hot wind.

Before Tyler even reached the counter, with its splayed out steaks and chops, its mounds of ground meat speckled with white flecks of fat, and one horrifyingly large beef tongue, the butcher was glaring at him.

"What do you want?" he asked.

"Uh . . ." Tyler reached into his pocket for the shopping list. *I should have had it ready*, he thought.

"I'm dying of old age while you make me wait!" Mr. Schmatzler screamed. "Hurry up, boy. It's closing time!" He flipped a switch, turning off the light in the meat case. The early-evening winter darkness spilled in through the front door.

Tyler repeated his "uh." The meaningless grunt morphed into a gasp as he searched through his pocket. He had the money. But the list was gone.

Tyler glanced back over his shoulder. *I dropped it.* The list was on the sidewalk. He was sure of that. "I'll be right back." He turned toward the door.

"Stop!" Mr. Schmatzler screamed. "I'm closing in ten seconds." He flicked another switch, killing half the ceiling lights.

Tyler spun back. *I can do it,* he told himself. He'd seen the list. He tried to picture the words in his mind. He knew what his mother wanted. Steak. Some kind of steak. "Uh, a pound, no, wait, a pound and a half of . . ."

What kind of steak was it?

Mr. Schmatzler yanked off his blood-splattered apron, threw it to the floor, and stormed around the counter. "I've had enough for one day!"

Tyler flinched. But the man blasted right past him and headed for the door.

"Delmonico!" Tyler shouted, remembering the name. "Delmonico steaks."

But the butcher was already past him and on his way out the door. "I'll give you some time to think," he said. He hit a final switch, high up above the top of the window, then stepped out and slammed the door behind himself.

Tyler looked at the butcher case, thought about what his mother would say if he returned without the meat, and then looked out the door just as the butcher locked it.

Click.

"Wait!" Tyler screamed.

But the man headed down the street.

Tyler ran to the door and yanked at it. It was locked tight. He yanked harder. It didn't matter.

"Come back!"

His words bounced off the door. Tyler stood, gasping to catch his breath.

Smack.

The sound came from behind him, like two muddy hands clapping together just once.

Tyler spun toward the meat case. It was too dark to see anything. He turned back to the door and stretched up, but the light switch was out of reach. Even with his best jump, he fell short. He looked at the other switch, behind the meat case. He started to inch his way toward it.

Smack. The sound shot from inside the case.

"Stop! You're just dead meat!" Tyler yelled. "You aren't alive."

He rushed past the case and flipped the switch on the back wall. The light flickered on, washing away the darkness.

In the movies, light banished horror and brought hope. In the butcher shop, light banished hope and brought horror.

Tyler could see everything now. The meat was pulling together, gathering into one large, wet, red mass of muscle and sinew. Steaks, chops, cutlets, even the ground beef—the meat was merging into a single creature. It formed a crude cylinder, the size of a small boy. The whole tube pulsed, as if it were somehow breathing.

Tyler backed against the wall. A ripping sound tore through the silence. A bone jutted out from the side of the tube, near one end, slanting downward so it touched the bottom of the case.

A second bone thrust out opposite the first. Two more burst through at the other end. The bones scratched against the bottom of the case, as if trying to gain traction.

The meat pulled itself to the rear of the case, pressed against the glass until it slid open, then fell out the back. It hit the floor with a splat. Tyler felt moist droplets shower his face. He could smell stale blood now. The rancid tang made his eyes burn.

He raced to the door and threw himself against it, not caring if he got cut when the glass smashed.

The door held.

"No! Let me out!" He threw himself against it harder, ramming it with his shoulder. The whole door rattled, but nothing broke.

Behind him, he heard the scrape of bones against the wooden floor. He didn't want to see what was there, but he had to look. The creature reminded him of an animal that had been poorly skinned with a dull knife. Meat had slid down to cover most of the four protruding bones, creating crude legs. A head of some sort had started to form. It was mostly a sphere, with a gaping opening in front, cushioning the drooping beef tongue.

Chips of bone lined the top and bottom of the opening, forming teeth. The tongue pulled back and the mouth snapped shut. The clack of bone striking bone shot through the air. The mouth gaped open again.

Tyler screamed, took two steps backwards, then threw himself at the door with all his strength.

The glass shattered. Tyler tumbled through the opening, landing hard on the sidewalk. A sharp pain shot through his left wrist. Lesser pains washed over his knees where they had struck the pavement.

Tyler pushed himself to his feet, wincing at the jolts of agony radiating from his wrist. That's when he saw the blood. His right leg had been slashed by the glass. The cut wasn't deep, but the skin had flapped open.

The creature dragged itself outside. Tyler tried to run, but his ankle betrayed him. He dropped back to his knees.

The creature moved across the sidewalk, leaving a smeared red trail of raw, shredded meat. When it reached Tyler, it rose up. The bone-lined mouth gaped wider. The creature was poised like a snake preparing to strike.

"Please . . . no . . ." Tyler held out a hand.

The creature paused. The head tilted toward the gash in his leg, then inched lower until it was hovering just inches above Tyler's torn flesh.

The mouth moved. The words were soft but clear.

"One of us." The creature turned and moved back toward the butcher shop, adding a second layer to the smeared trail. "The little monster is one of us."

As Tyler watched it walk to the door, he recognized something. He rolled to his knees, reached out, and grabbed a slab of meat from the side of the creature. "Delmonico steak," he said. That's what his mother had sent him for.

Slowly, making sure he didn't overstress his ankle, Tyler got to his feet. Clutching the dead meat in his hand, the live meat hobbled home.

MY NEW HAT

Mom took me to Fairbrink's Department Store for a new winter hat, because my old one was worn out. The old hat would have lasted longer, but kids were always snatching it from my head and throwing it around. Then, when they got tired of that, they'd toss my hat in the road right when a bus was coming along. So it got run over a lot. I guess that was better than having them toss me around.

I figured I should look for a sturdier hat this time.

"Here's a nice one, Daniel," Mom said, holding up a knitted hat made of dark green wool.

"It's nice, but I want something warmer." I couldn't tell her I wanted something that could survive bullies and bus tires. If she knew how much I got picked on, she'd get all worried and go talk to the principal. She doesn't understand bullies, and how things work in school. But she understands staying warm. I kept looking, hoping I could find the perfect hat. And there it was, sticking out from under a pile of felt hats on a discount table.

I grabbed it and gave it a tug. It was leather. Real leather. I could tell by the smell. It looked sort of like the helmets you see in pictures of ancient college football games, back when the players wore short pants and funny shirts. I tried it on. It was really tight. Great. Between the slick surface and the tight fit, kids would have a hard time snatching it from my head.

"I like this one," I told Mom.

"Are you sure?" She picked up a red plaid cap with earflaps. "This looks warmer."

It looked like a red flag, with the words PUNCH ME on it. "Nah. I really like this one." I pulled it down even tighter. It was wonderfully smooth, with nothing to grab on to. "It's exactly what I need."

So she bought it for me. The next day, I put on my new hat, along with my coat and gloves, and headed out for the bus stop, which was two blocks from my house.

They were there. The bullies. Frankie, Stan, Ivan, and the others.

"Look at the dork!" Frankie shouted. He wasn't wearing anything on his head. I was pretty sure there wasn't anything inside his head, either, but I kept that thought to myself.

Stan barked out a laugh and tried to grab my hat. His fingers slipped off the leather. I hoped that would convince him to stop trying, but it just made him angry. "Come here!" he shouted.

I backed away. Right up against a tree. All of them moved toward me, their eyes glowing in anticipation. I had a feeling they would be just as happy to remove my hat by ripping off my head. Stan grabbed the collar of my jacket in one meaty fist.

That's when the shadow fell over us.

I looked up.

Something large and flat and round was hovering right over our heads. It was a flying saucer.

We all scattered as it moved toward the ground.

The saucer touched down in the middle of the road. I wasn't under it anymore—I was ten or fifteen feet away—but I was too amazed to move any farther. So was everyone else.

A hatch opened beneath the saucer, making a ramp.

An alien came down. He had two arms and two legs, just like us. But he had gigantic eyes, and a round head. The top of his head was smooth and brown, like leather.

Three more aliens came out behind him. They each carried some sort of device that looked like a trumpet made of glass and silver.

They pointed the flared ends at us. Before we could move, Frankie and the others vanished in puffs of smoke.

It smelled like when something gets burned in the bottom of the toaster oven.

The aliens looked at me. I hoped it wouldn't hurt too much when they zapped me. But instead of shooting me, they lowered their weapons. And then they knelt. They bowed until their heads touched the ground—their smooth, brown, leather-like heads.

Then they led me onto their ship, making high-pitched sounds that I later learned were songs of joy. They were thrilled to discover me. Now, they spend all their time finding ways to please and entertain me. They've taken me all around the galaxy in their amazing ship. I've visited hundreds of incredible planets. The spacemen do whatever I tell them. And they give me whatever I ask for. Somehow, they understand me when I talk. I'm their ruler now. That's pretty cool. Except I have a feeling I'd better never take off my hat. But that's okay. I really do like it.

FABRICATIONS

Wellington Portsmith III had more money than anyone else in our class. I knew this because he pretty much shoved it in our faces every day. I'm not poor. I have nice clothes and several pairs of shoes. And if I were poor, I'd be okay with that. There's more to life than stuff. Sunshine is free. So are books, if you have a library card.

But it wasn't fun getting constant Wellington-is-wealthy reports throughout the day. He'd make a big deal out of pulling his expensive gold pen out of the pocket of his shirt and opening his leather-covered notebook.

It was bad enough when he mostly showed off to the boys in our class. But then he started trying to impress all of us girls. Yesterday, as we were taking our seats at the start of the day, he tapped the cuff of Holly Milborn's blouse and said, "Polyester?"

She ignored him, but he didn't stop. He patted his chest. "Silk. Pure silk. I never wear anything synthetic."

He babbled a bit more about his linen pants and leather shoes. I tuned him out. After he took his seat, I told Holly, "I like your clothes."

"Thanks," she said. But I could tell she was upset.

After school, I went to see Dad at work. I can visit him anytime I want, because he's the boss. He has his own company. But he just started it last year, so there's not a lot of money coming in. As I said, that's okay. Dad isn't trying to get rich. He's trying to help people by coming up with new kinds of medicine. He does that by splicing genes. In some ways, it's pretty complicated. But in other ways, it's amazingly simple.

Consider this. Some people have a problem with high blood sugar. We all have bacteria in our stomachs. But not the kind of bacteria that eat sugar. So, what if you could take the gene in a sugar-eating bacteria that gives it a sweet tooth, and put that craving into the DNA of the bacteria in our stomachs. Now they'd eat sugar.

As Dad would say, that's an oversimplification. A lot of things could go wrong. And you have to be incredibly careful when you're making medicine or modifying genes.

But I was going to splice up something that wouldn't be a danger to anyone. At least, not a physical danger. Though, if my plan worked, it would produce some serious psychological damage. First, I had to get permission.

"Can I use the sequencer?" I asked.

Dad looked up from the eyepiece of his optical microscope. "What for?"

Here was the moment of truth. I could try to hide my plan from Dad. I'd feel guilty if I did that. Or I could tell him the truth and hope he didn't stop me.

I explained everything.

Dad listened until I was finished. He's good at that. He always lets me speak. He never interrupts. When I was done, he said, "We absolutely have to run safety tests before anything leaves this building."

It took me a second to realize the full meaning of this. "So you're saying yes?"

"It seems like a good learning experience—for both of you."

"Yay!" I'll admit, I leaped up a bit and clapped my hands like a schoolgirl. Of course, I *was* a schoolgirl, so I guess it was okay to act like one once in a while. But then I grabbed a lab coat and switched to young-scientist mode. Though this young scientist will admit to letting out a giggle or two while she worked.

It took a week to overcome all the snags that popped up. But it was worthwhile. When I was finished, everything tested perfectly.

Next Monday, I brought a small piece of cotton to school, inside a corked test tube.

I had a tiny moment of doubt as I walked toward our classroom. *It is kind of mean*, I thought. But then, right ahead of me, I saw Wellington standing by his locker.

As Holly and two other girls walked past him, he sneered and said, "What'd you do—sew that yourself from plastic bags?"

They sped down the hall.

"Egyptian cotton," he said, tapping his shirt. "And linen," he added, pointing to his pants.

I pulled the cork from the test tube, grabbed the damp piece of cotton, and rubbed my fingers over it. Then I walked up to Wellington, touched his sleeve, and said, "Nice."

"How would you know?" he said, pulling his arm away. "You're dressed like you made your clothes from tossed-out candy wrappers."

"I guess I don't know much of anything," I said as I fought back my grin and walked away from him.

I'd done all the calculations earlier, but I couldn't help running the figures in my head as I took my seat in homeroom. Happily, the school routine is pretty much the same every day.

Five minutes after the late bell, the morning announcements started. It was hard to keep from staring at Wellington. But I knew there'd be nothing to see yet.

There'd be a lot to see real soon.

After greeting us over the speaker, the principal asked us to stand for the pledge of allegiance.

Be patient, I told myself. Even if it happened after we sat, it would be good. But it would be awesome if it happened before that.

". . . with liberty and justice for all."

As the last words rose from the class, I heard a startled shout from behind me.

"Hey!"

I turned toward the screamer, like the rest of the class. Unlike the rest of the class, I knew who was screaming and, even better, why he was screaming.

"What—?" Wellington was staring at his sleeve. It hung from his arm in shreds, as if he'd been mauled by a couple wild dogs.

"It worked!" I was excited enough to speak out loud, but smart enough to keep my voice to a whisper.

Nobody noticed that I'd spoken. They were all watching Wellington's shirt fall apart. The bacteria I had created had a hunger for natural fabrics. They reproduced rapidly, and traveled only by physical contact. They also had a very short life span.

Wellington's shirt was gone. His pants had started to disintegrate.

"Ahhhg!" He spun around, apparently unsure what to do.

Spinning is a bad idea when your clothes are barely held together. Centrifugal force is pretty interesting. Stopping quickly after a spin is another bad idea, especially when one takes inertia into account. Wellington pretty much pantsed himself.

At this point, he came to his senses enough to realize it would be a good idea to flee the room.

As he shot through the door, I noticed that his underwear must also be made of a natural fabric. But the less said about that, the better.

By the time his mom brought him a change of clothes, all the bacteria would have died off.

I'll admit, I almost felt bad for him. Especially when he transferred to another school. But I felt good for the rest of us. Until the new girl came, who put everyone else down because she had the nicest hair.

Hair would be tougher. Especially since I had to come up with something that targeted just one person. That's not a problem. I loved a challenge.

PLAGUE YOUR EYES

Gilroy headed for the library. He had a book report due the next day. But he had no plans to read the book. Books were stupid. There was no way Gilroy was going to waste his free time reading one. Not when he could play games.

But the last time he'd skipped a book report, his parents got angry enough to threaten to take away his games and movies. That wouldn't do. A month ago, at the same time Gilroy had skipped his report, his friend Gordon Larmuller had found a book report on the Internet. Gordon cut-and-pasted it into Word, put his name on it, printed out a copy, and handed it in. That wasn't a good idea. It turned out teachers have a way to check for copied stuff.

But they can only check for things that are on the Internet, Gilroy realized. That's where Gordon had gone wrong. So Gilroy figured he just had to find a book report that wasn't anywhere online. He lived three blocks away from the community college. There had to be something in the library. Something he could take for his own.

"I have to do a book report," he told the librarian.

"When is it due?" she asked.

"To—" Gilroy caught himself before he said *tomorrow*. "Two weeks." He smiled at the clever way he'd kept from revealing the truth. "I need a good book."

"There are a lot of them to choose from," the librarian said. "Anyone who lives in the county can check out books from here. What do you like to read?"

"Actually, I was hoping I could read what other people thought about a book," he said. "That would be a good idea, wouldn't it?"

"That would be an excellent idea." The librarian seemed thrilled by this. "Come over here." She walked toward a shelf near the far corner of the library. "This has literary criticism. You're welcome to browse. But if you want some suggestions—"

"I'll browse," Gilroy said. "Thanks."

She left him there, with a towering shelf of already-written assignments.

"Score!" Gilroy whispered as soon as the librarian had returned to her desk. He might never have to do homework again. At least not for book reports. Maybe not for history, either.

It took him almost an hour to find what he needed, but it was worth it. He took the book to the photocopier. A big sign on top of the machine warned that it wasn't okay to make copies of whole books. Gilroy had no plans to do that. He just needed the one essay.

After he'd finished making the copy, he found the actual book the essay discussed and went to check it out. He didn't need it, but he didn't want the librarian to get suspicious. He figured he'd need her help again, now that he'd discovered this treasure trove of ready-made papers.

As soon as he got home, he went on the computer and checked to see if the essay existed anywhere online. He put in the author's name and the title. No hits. The author's name came up for some other stuff, including several books. He was an old guy with frizzy white hair and a tiny mustache, who wasn't even around anymore. No surprise. The essay had been written about fifty years ago.

"Perfect. Nobody will know." Gilroy typed the paper into his computer. He even changed a couple big words, like *ostentatious* and *predetermined* because he knew his teacher wouldn't believe he'd ever use them. And she'd be right.

The next morning, he handed in his paper. The next night, he awoke from a deep sleep to find a man with frizzy white hair and a small mustache standing in his room.

Gilroy let out a scream.

"You stole my words," the man said.

"No, I didn't!" Gilroy shouted, though he had no idea how to back up the lie. "Go away!" He heard his parents running down the hall toward his bedroom.

"Now, I'll steal yours," the man said. He reached out and touched Gilroy's throat with fingers as cold as wet snow and as dry as the pages of ancient books.

Gilroy's door flew open. His parents raced into the room just as the man faded from sight.

"What's wrong?" his mother asked.

I'll tell them it was a bad dream, Gilroy thought. Even when terrified, he was a genius at lies. Gilroy tried to speak, but no words came out. He tried again. Nothing. His words had been stolen. Nobody other than Gilroy would really care about that. While stealing from a book was a serious violation, taking Gilroy's words was really little more than petty theft.

CONTROL ISSUES

If you don't have a lot of cash, Game Pit is the best store on the planet. They sell used stuff cheap. That's especially great for me, because I have an old system—a PS2—and it's hard to find games. They don't sell new PS2 games many places, and I don't think anybody even makes them anymore, but Game Pit keeps a good stock of the old ones.

I was at the store with my friend Chase, looking through a bin of used hardware when I found the coolest thing of all. It was a wireless controller. I know that's not a big deal now. Every system comes with wireless controllers. But back when the PS2 came out, the regular controllers had cords, so you had to sit pretty close to the TV. I don't mind being close, but our couch is on the other side of the room from the TV. It would be nice to really be a couch potato, and not a rug potato.

"Check it out!" I said, holding up the plastic bag that had the controller and the receiver. "Wireless."

"Sweet," Chase said. "We should see if there's another." He started rooting through the bin. We play games at my place a lot. I figured it would have been awesome to find a second one.

We didn't find another controller, so I took the one I had up to the register and paid for it.

"You need batteries?" Chase asked.

"I don't know." I took the controller out of the bag and popped open the battery compartment. "Nope. It has some. I wonder if they're dead?" Just to make sure they worked, I pressed the power switch. The little red light between the START and SELECT buttons came on. I was all set. We headed to my place. I figured Chase and I could take turns using the wireless controller.

We'd just reached my front door when I looked down at the bag. "Oh no!"

"What's wrong?" Chase asked.

I held up the bag. "The receiver isn't there. I think it fell out." I'd torn a pretty big hole in the side of the bag when I took out the controller.

"That's not good."

"We have to go back and look for it." Without the receiver, which plugged into a joystick port on the PS2, the controller was worthless.

Chase and I walked back toward the store, scanning the sidewalk for the receiver. We'd only gone two blocks when I spotted trouble ahead of us. Donald Blotzman and a couple of his thug friends were heading our way.

"Uh-oh," Chase said.

"Let's cross the street. We can get back to searching after he's gone."

Before I could move, I heard one of Donald's friends say, "Hey—what's this?"

He bent down and picked up something from the edge of the sidewalk. Even from a block away, I could tell it was the receiver.

"It's mine. That's what it is," Donald said. He snatched it from the other kid's hand, stared at it for a minute, then shoved it in the back pocket of his jeans.

"Oh, this is just wonderful," I said. "It's gone for sure. I can't ask him for it. If he knows I want it, he'll never let it go." I looked at the controller in my hand. It was worthless now.

"It's no use to him," Chase said. "You never know. Maybe he'll give it to you."

"He'll give it to me, all right," I said. "With his fists."

"Come on, what's the worst that could happen?" Chase asked.

"The worst? A broken nose. A broken neck. Broken ribs. You want me to go on?"

"I'm tired of being scared," Chase said. "I'm going to ask him for it."

"No!"

But it was too late. Chase was already headed for Donald. I followed him, but didn't catch up.

"Hey, you know that thing you picked up," Chase said when he reached Donald. "It belongs to—"

"Out of my way," Donald said. He gave Chase a push.

I expected Chase to give up. Instead, after staggering back a step or two, he moved right in front of Donald. "I wasn't finished," he said.

"You are totally finished," Donald said. He grabbed Chase's shirt in one large fist and pulled back his other fist to throw a punch.

I flinched. But I decided to try to help. There was no way I could reach them before Donald threw the first punch. But I could at least get there before the second or third one. Not that I was sure I could do anything more useful than convincing Donald to hit me instead, or helping Chase pick up his teeth.

I clenched my fists, wondering whether it would hurt more to get hit by Donald or to hit him on his hard head.

To my credit, I kept moving.

Donald, on the other hand, froze. I don't mean he paused. I mean he had stopped moving. He still had a grip on Chase, and he still had his other fist drawn back. But he wasn't moving at all. He wasn't blinking or breathing.

I stared at Donald for a moment. Then I looked down at my hand. I was clutching the controller. My thumb was pressed against the START button. In most games, START works as a pause button.

Chase's eyes were squeezed shut. I couldn't blame him. He probably figured Donald was purposely not hitting him yet, just to make him suffer for longer.

I tapped START again. Donald's fist shot forward. I barely managed to pause him again before he hit Chase.

Okay—this could be good. As long as I could think fast. I still had Donald's two friends to worry about. For the moment, they were staring, too. But they probably weren't going to stand there forever.

I had to do this perfectly, and hope I guessed right. If I was wrong, Chase's head would end up with a couple of knuckle-shaped dents. Luckily, I was a pretty good game player. Okay—that's being modest. I was really good. If I owned a new system, I'd be on tons of leader boards. But my PS2 skills should be good enough for what I had to do.

I shifted my grip on the controller, holding it like I was

playing a game, with a thumb on each of the two sticks. I slid my right thumb over to hit START, unpaused Donald, tapped B, which most games use to drop things, then threw both sticks left. Donald let go of Chase and spun counterclockwise. I wasn't sure which way he'd spin, since some games reverse the *x* axis of the camera, but it didn't matter, since there was someone on each side.

Donald and Chase both yelled in surprise. Donald finished throwing his punch, taking out one of his pals. I turned him around 180 degrees, so he faced his other friend, and hit the X button, which is the one most of my games use for melee attacks. Donald threw another punch. The other bully went down.

Just for fun, I hit A. Yup, it made him jump. I hit START when he was in the air. His body froze, but he still came down. It would have been pretty amazing to freeze him in midair, but I guess the laws of physics are pretty unbreakable.

"What just happened?" Chase asked.

Instead of answering, I put Donald through a short dance, leaping and spinning like a third-grader trying to do the *Nutcracker.* Then I paused him. I noticed that words appeared on his shirt, like on a pause screen.

"That's awesome," Chase said. "Thanks for saving my skin."

"No problem. But, bully or not, I guess it's wrong to keep him paused forever. How am I going to get the receiver? If I can't control him, he's going to murder both of us."

"You could leave it in his pocket. He'd never bully us again."

"Until he changes his pants," I said.

"That could be months."

"Seriously, what do you think we should do."

A car whizzed past. Chase stared out at the street for a moment, then said, "I have an idea."

I knew him well enough to read his thoughts, especially when they were so obvious. "No way. We're not making him walk in front of a car." I forced myself not to smile. I guess I was evil enough to like the idea, but not evil enough to actually do it. I wonder if that made me mid-evil.

"What about a motorcycle?" Chase asked. "He'd probably just break a leg."

"Forget it."

"Bicycle?"

"Nope."

"Skater?"

"No."

"I'm all out of ideas," Chase said.

"Me, too." I looked at the two guys on the ground. There was no way to know how long it would be before they woke up. I definitely didn't want to be around when that happened.

"Did you see this?" Chase asked, pointing to Donald's shirt.

"Yeah. It's a pause menu." Every game had one. I scanned down it, and got as far as the third listing.

RESUME
CONTROLS
DIFFICULTY

"Difficulty!" I shouted.

RESUME was highlighted. I pressed down twice on the crosspad. Then I hit X to select DIFFICULTY. The text changed.

EASY
NORMAL

DIFFICULT
BERSERK

At the moment, BERSERK was highlighted. I selected EASY, then backed out of the menu, all the way to the main pause screen.

"Ready?" I asked Chase.

"Yeah. Do it."

I unpaused Donald.

"I'm going to murder you!" he shouted.

He lunged toward me and swung a fist.

I couldn't believe how slowly he moved. I stepped aside. His fist clipped my shoulder. It felt like I'd been smacked with an understuffed pillow swung by a toddler.

I gave him a push. He toppled over. I bent down, slipped the receiver out of his pocket, and stepped back. He got to his feet and rushed toward me again.

"Let's go," I said.

Chase and I walked off. Donald ran after us, but it didn't look like he'd be able to catch up. I could no longer control him, but it didn't matter. He was permanently set on EASY. I had a feeling a lot of his usual victims would be in for a big surprise the next time he tried to bully them.

"Well, that worked out a lot better than I expected," Chase said.

"Remind me to buy more batteries," I said.

"Why?"

"There are a lot of other bullies out there. I'd hate to lose power now that I finally have some."

MR. CHOMPYWOMP

Alina clutched the teddy bear close to her as she walked toward her aunt's apartment. It was on the same block as her own apartment building. She didn't have to cross the street to get there—she just had to turn the corner twice. That was nice, because it meant she could head off in either direction and not get lost. Her mother would have walked with her, but there'd been an emergency. Alina didn't really understand what had happened. She just knew that nice old Mrs. Pershing, across the hall, had been frantic, and there'd been a lot of shouting and screaming. Then, Alina's mom had knelt down and said to her, "You need to go to your auntie's. Can you walk there by yourself?"

Alina had nodded. She wasn't afraid of anything. Not when she had Mr. Chompywomp with her. He would protect her from anything. That was her secret.

"Don't talk to anyone," her mother said.

"I won't."

"Don't even look at anyone."

"I know."

Alina grabbed the teddy bear from her bed, kissed her mom, and took the elevator down to the first floor.

She headed out, clutching the teddy bear close so that Mr. Chompywomp would hear her heart beating.

Left or right?

Still clutching the teddy bear with both arms, she headed left. Her heart sped up as she turned the corner and saw the boys. Three of them. Older, tougher, and obviously looking for trouble. She froze, wondering whether she could retreat before they noticed her.

"What's this?" the biggest one said, stepping in front of her. He had the name CALVIN stitched on his jacket.

Another of the boys stepped past Calvin and moved behind her. The third stood where he was, off to the side.

"You lost?" Calvin asked.

Alina shook her head. She didn't see anybody else nearby to rescue her.

"You must be lost. Anyone who lives here knows you gotta pay tribute to King Calvin. Got any money?"

Alina shook her head again.

"You don't say much. Maybe I'll talk to him instead." Calvin snatched the teddy bear.

"Don't hurt Mr. Chompywomp!" she shouted before she could control herself.

Calvin let out a laugh that had no humor in it. "Mr. Chompywomp?" He squeezed the bear's neck and prodded its mouth with his other hand. "No teeth. No real mouth. How's he gonna chomp anything?"

Alina kept her own mouth shut.

"What a piece of junk," Calvin said. "He's not even sewn together good." He yanked at the bear's head. It separated with a rip. Loose threads dangled from the ragged neck.

"Oh, poor little bear," the boy behind Alina said.

"Looks like Mr. Chompywomp came apart," Calvin said. "I wonder if your head is attached any better."

"That's not Mr. Chompywomp," Alina said. "That's Mr. Bear." She figured she wasn't revealing a secret. At least, not a secret that would be kept much longer.

Calvin stood there, not showing any sign of understanding.

"Mr. Chompywomp lives inside Mr. Bear. Until he gets hungry."

Something dark and strong burst from the open neck of Mr. Bear and leaped onto Calvin's chest. Calvin's scream drowned out the wet sound of Mr. Chompywomp digging for his heart.

Before Calvin even hit the ground, Mr. Chompywomp had leaped to his second victim. The third one fell soon after.

Alina waited until Mr. Chompywomp had groomed the blood from his fur before letting him crawl back into Mr. Bear.

"Don't worry," she said as she walked away from King Calvin and his friends. "Auntie has a sewing kit. I'll fix you up as good as new." But, like always, she'd make sure not to sew Mr. Bear's head on too tightly. Mr. Chompywomp had a big appetite. Luckily, King Calvin wasn't the only heartless person out there.

FLESH DRIVE

It's bad enough I got ear infections all the time. It was even worse my parents were too cheap to pay for an operation in the United States. They decided to drag me to this sketchy hospital in South America that was selling a combination vacation/surgery package.

So, basically, I had a good shot at dying at the hands of some doctors who got their medical school degrees on the Internet, but my parents would both get a great tan.

Luckily, through some miracle, the doctors didn't kill me when they were carving into my head. It wasn't until a month later that I noticed the weird part. When my scalp finally healed, and the last piece of scab fell off, I saw something small and metallic on the side of my head. I spotted it when I was brushing my teeth.

I leaned closer to the mirror and stared. I'd recognize that small trapezoidal shape anywhere. So would every kid on the planet who owned a single piece of modern electronics that used memory cards.

It was a USB port.

No way.

I touched it. It felt hard and cold. That didn't tell me anything. But I definitely recognized it. I used a USB cable to transfer files to my gaming systems and to my parents' camera, which currently contained a couple gigs' worth of photos of them having fun on the beach.

I went back to my room. I had Dad's old computer. He was as cheap with electronics as he was with surgery, so the PC was pretty ancient. I was probably the only kid on the block using a version of Windows that was more than three releases out of date. Still, the PC wasn't so old that it didn't have USB ports. I grabbed my cable from the drawer and stood there for a long time. I wasn't sure whether I should risk it. But, hey, I'd survived that hospital. I felt I could survive anything.

I plugged myself in.

A small window popped up above the task bar. MASS STORAGE DEVICE DETECTED.

For sure. I opened the MY COMPUTER window and looked at the devices. The hard drive was there in C, the CD-ROM drive in B, and the floppy in A. (That's how old the PC was. It had a floppy drive and couldn't play DVDs.) Listed below those, I saw E: MASS STORAGE DEVICE.

Cool. I right-clicked on PROPERTIES. Wow. My brain had a capacity of 1,000 terabytes. Then I saw it was only using about 50 terabytes. I clicked on the icon. It showed two folders: SHORT TERM, LONG TERM.

I opened LONG TERM. That had dozens of folders. I found a folder for LANGUAGE. Just for fun, I opened the drive on my computer and grabbed the dictionary file. I dragged it over to my brain.

Here goes.

I released the mouse button so the file would copy into the LANGUAGE folder. As the progress bar filled, I tried to see whether my mind had changed. It was hard to tell. I had a book on my desk. I flipped it opened and looked for a word I shouldn't know. I didn't see anything. But maybe that was because I knew all the words.

I looked across the room at my bookcase. My summer reading assignment was there. That would definitely be filled with words I'd never heard of. I could thumb through it and really test my brain. I got up from my desk and headed across the room.

I'd only taken a single step when I felt the tug.

Oh, no. I'd forgotten about the USB port. A thought shot through my mind as I reached toward my head to keep the cable from pulling out. I'd yanked a flash drive out of my computer once, without ejecting it first. The whole thing had been fried. All the memory was gone. Every byte had been erased.

As I reached up, I felt the free end of the cable hit my hand. I was too

GOTHIC HORRORS

The three witches, Selena thought as she looked across the cafeteria at the goth girls. Mimi, Amanda, and Katerina were dressed as darkly as the school would allow, in black tops, fishnet sleeves, and black skirts over black tights. A splash of red cloth here or there contrasted with black fingernails and black lips. Their eyes peered from dark hollows of makeup.

They were gloomy, sulky, and indistinguishable. They were morose and threatening. They were also everything Selena wanted to be. Witches. Princesses of Darkness. Whatever they were, Selena found herself drawn to them. They were the most real girls in the school, not seeming to care what anybody thought about them. Not afraid to be themselves.

But they'd ignored her awkward attempts to enter their circle. She'd tried talking to them at their lockers. They'd stared at her as if she spoke Latin. She'd tried hovering nearby when they gathered outside after school. They'd looked right through her. They weren't interested. She didn't matter.

The bell rang. Selena watched as students untangled

themselves from the benches on each side of the long tables and jostled toward the doorway. The jocks laughed and punched each other. The nerds laughed and tried to punch each other. The pretty girls teased the cute guys. The punks sneered and looked bored. The goth girls looked as if their best friends, or maybe their pets, had recently died in tragic and horrible ways.

Amanda and Katerina grabbed their purses, which were also black. Amanda dropped her books as she was gathering them, and Mimi bent to help her. When the three girls left, Selena noticed Mimi's purse on the seat. She walked over to their table and waited for the cafeteria to empty out. Soon, nobody was left except for a custodian, who was busy wiping down tables and cursing the sloppiness of the students.

The purse, black cloth with an open clasp, lay on the seat, gaping wide enough to display a tangle of contents. *I should bring it to her,* Selena thought. She reached down and imagined Mimi thanking her when she returned the purse. Mimi would actually look at her—not through her. Then Mimi would ask her to hang out with them.

The fantasy was replaced with another, darker scene where Mimi snatched the purse from her hands and accused her of theft, spewing screams at her. Selena pulled herself away from the daydreams and gazed at the purse. Something dark jutted out, as if trying to escape. Nail polish. Black polish.

Her parents would never let her use it. But her parents worked late most school days. She could paint her nails now, enjoy them for the rest of the day, and remove the polish before her parents got home. Selena sat at the table and put her hand on the bottle. She had a study hall this period. She could risk being a couple minutes late.

She uncapped the polish and painted the thick, black liquid on her nails. The polish dried to a beautiful, glossy darkness. As Selena slipped the bottle back into the bag, she sensed someone behind her. She swung her legs around and stood, to find herself facing Mimi.

"I didn't . . ." Selena tried to think what action she needed to deny. *I didn't take anything?* Almost true. *I didn't hurt anything?* Very true.

"It's okay," Mimi said. She picked up the purse, then looked down toward Selena's hands. "It's not about the nails." She reached into her purse and removed a small silver tube. "Are you sure this is what you want?"

Selena nodded.

"Stand still."

While Selena stood, Mimi painted Selena's lips.

"Thank you," Selena said when Mimi was done.

"It's not about the lips or the clothes, either," Mimi said. "It's not about appearances. It's about being your true self." She took her purse and walked away.

Selena headed for her study hall, but stopped on the way to look at herself in the girls' room mirror.

She pushed her hair back and turned her head slowly from side to side. She liked what she saw. *This is my true self,* she thought. She lacked eye shadow, but that could be taken care of next time. She also lacked black hair. Hers was dark brown. But maybe she could make one little change at a time, keeping each one small enough so her parents never noticed.

She left the bathroom, and ran straight into her English teacher.

"Selena!" Mrs. Pelter said, her face contorting in horror. "What happened to your lips? You look awful."

"Mimi made me do it!" Selena blurted out. Her fear of Mrs. Pelter's disapproval destroyed her sense of honor. As she heard her own words, she flinched and bit her lip. The lipstick tasted oddly bitter.

"Did her friends help her? Were those other two girls involved?"

Selena knew there was still a chance to take back what she'd said. *They didn't make me do anything. I asked Mimi. It was my idea.* No—she thought back. *Mimi offered me the lipstick. I didn't ask for it.*

Mrs. Pelter seemed to take her silence as agreement. "I'll certainly see that the principal has a talk with them," she said. "We do not tolerate bullying in our school."

She stormed off, leaving Selena with one last tiny chance to call after her and fix things.

Selena turned the other way and walked to her study hall. *I should have said something.* But Mimi, Amanda, and Katerina got in trouble all the time. One more mark against them wouldn't make any real difference.

Mrs. Pelter might have reacted with revulsion, but the students in her study hall, and in her other classes, seemed fascinated by her new look. They stared at her and whispered to each other.

I've made an impression, Selena thought. She responded to their stares with an empty gaze that she hoped showed no emotion at all. She decided that she would practice it in the mirror when she got home.

On the way out of the building after her last class, Selena saw the thee girls leaving the principal's office. Mimi stared at her with an icy coldness that sent a chill up Selena's back and down her arms.

Selena tried to stare back. *Maybe I'll start my own group,* she thought.

Mimi raised the first two fingers of each hand, forming a pair of vee shapes. So did Katerina and Amanda. Each girl interlaced her fingers. Still staring at Selena, they spoke one by one. Katerina, Amanda, and finally Mimi each chanted a line.

A false fourth betrays true sisters, three,
So three by four your punishment will be;
Twelve horrors to repay your treachery.

A hot wind blew through the hallway, flapping the edges of their black garments and swirling their hair. Selena turned and fled. Her face flushed with a mix of fear and guilt.

But when she got home and looked at her reflection in the small mirror in the hallway, her guilt melted and her fear gave way to excitement. She loved what she saw. *I can do this,* she thought. If she left for school a bit earlier than usual, she could put on makeup when she got there. And she could take it off when she got home. Maybe she could even change her clothes. Or wear black underneath a shirt or sweater she could remove after she left her house. She could make it work.

She went up to her room, where she had a bigger mirror, and gave herself a gloomy stare. It was hard not to smile. "I've finally found who I am," she said. "I'm true to myself."

She would draw others to her side. They'd follow her. Maybe, if they apologized, she'd even allow Mimi, Katerina, and Amanda into her group. But they'd have to beg for forgiveness first. Selena lost herself in fantasies until the sound of a car pulling into the driveway jolted her from her thoughts. She recognized the scraping noise her mother's car made when it turned to the right.

She's home.

Selena raced to the bathroom and grabbed nail polish remover and cotton balls from the drawer beneath the sink. She dabbed at her thumb and started to scrub, expecting to see a black smear on the cotton.

The remover failed to do anything.

Selena stared at her hand for a moment, then scrubbed another nail. No change.

She heard the front door open.

"I'm home," her mother called.

I can hide my hands, but she'll see my lips right away. Selena snatched a tissue from the box on the counter and wiped at her lips. The tissue came away clean.

"Where are you?" her mother called.

"In the bathroom." Selena kicked the door closed. Her fingertips tingled. As Selena stared at her hands, tiny black cracks spread from the sides of her nails.

The cracks displayed a frightening symmetry. Three spread out on each side of each nail, equally long and equally spaced.

When the cracks started to move, Selena realized they were something else.

"Legs . . . ," she whispered. The tiny, jointed legs pushed down hard against her cuticles, raising the beetle-black insect bodies from her fingertips. Selena screamed as her nails tore themselves free from her hands and fell to the floor. They scurried off, disappearing beneath the baseboard.

Twelve horrors to repay your treachery.

The words exploded in her mind as she stared at her ten damaged fingers. Beneath the scream, she realized her lips tingled. Selena clapped a hand across her mouth, then jerked it away in reaction to the cold, slimy feel that met her palm.

The mirror verified her fears. Two black, bloated, glossy worms wriggled as they ripped free of her face.

The bathroom door opened. There was a gasp. Selena's mother joined in with her own screams as she stared in horror at her daughter's lipless face.

On the floor, the black worms wriggled beneath the cabinet. Across town, Mimi, Katerina, and Amanda, hearing the whisper of an echo of a scream drifting in the wind, allowed themselves a small, fleeting smile.

IN A CLASS BY HIMSELF

"Hello, Justin. I'm your teacher, Mrs. Cromwell. Come on in and take a seat."

Justin stood in the doorway and looked around the classroom. This had to be the wrong place. He glanced down at the paper in his hand. *Mrs. Cromwell. Room 204.* He looked at the number painted on the open door. *204.*

"You must be the new student. Don't be shy," Mrs. Cromwell said. She smiled. "Hurry up. Choose a seat. You're just in time for math."

Justin walked into the room and looked at the rows of empty desks. As he passed the first row, he thought about sitting all the way in the back. That would be too far away if he was the only kid in the class. He settled for the second row, two seats in from the left side, near a window.

"All right, class, let's get to work," Mrs. Cromwell said. She walked to the blackboard and wrote a problem. "Let's see. Now, who would like to try this one?"

Justin looked to his left and his right. Beyond any doubt, he was alone with the teacher.

"Volunteers?" Mrs. Cromwell asked.

Justin sat there.

"If there aren't any volunteers, I'll have to pick someone."

Justin raised his hand.

"How nice. Come on up, Justin." Mrs. Cromwell held out the piece of chalk.

Justin went to the board and worked on the problem. It wasn't hard, and he was good at math. As he took his seat, Mrs. Cromwell wrote a second problem on the board.

"Now, who would like to try this one?" she asked.

Justin didn't raise his hand.

"Come, now. Don't be shy. It's not that hard."

Justin kept his hand down.

"Well, let's see. How about you, Justin? Come on up and give it a try."

Justin went to the board and solved the problem. He solved seven more problems before math was done. Then he got to read aloud—a whole lot—during the reading period.

"How was school?" Justin's mom asked when Justin got home.

"Different," he said.

"That's nice," his mother said, smiling as if Justin had given her one of his typical answers, like *fine* or *okay*.

The next day, nothing had changed. Mrs. Cromwell was up front, acting as if this were a perfectly normal situation, and Justin was facing her, getting taught all by himself.

"How was school?" his mother asked when he got home.

"Aardvark," Justin said, testing his suspicion.

"That's nice," his mom said. "Your birthday is coming up next week. I can make cupcakes. How many do you need?"

"Two," Justin said, figuring his teacher wouldn't want to be left out.

"Two?" his mom asked.

"I mean, two dozen," Justin said. For some reason, he didn't want to tell her he was the only student. He still hadn't figured out what it meant, and he was pretty sure it didn't mean anything his mom would want to know about.

"Anybody allergic to anything?" she asked.

"I don't think so."

On the way to school the next day, Justin came up with a theory. This was some kind of test. He wasn't sure what they were trying to find out about him, but that was the only explanation he'd thought of that came anywhere near close to making sense.

So, since he had no idea what sort of reaction they expected from him, he was going to make sure not to react at all. He decided to act as if there were nothing unusual about the situation, no matter how long he had to keep going to this class. If Mrs. Cromwell could pretend everything was normal, so could he.

His resolve lasted nearly a month. Finally, after an entire week filled with group activities where he had to carry out all the parts—the play was especially difficult—Justin realized he couldn't take any more.

I'm done, he told himself as he watched the clock tick toward the end of the day. *I can't take another week of this. I don't care what they do to me.*

He sat in his seat, took a deep breath, and got ready to tell his teacher all of this.

"I'm done! I can't take another day of this!"

Justin's jaw dropped open as he stared at his teacher and listened to her shouting.

"I don't care what they do to me," Mrs. Cromwell added as she stormed out of the room. "This is absurd."

The bell rang. Justin went home.

"How was school?" his mom asked.

"Snarflegrub," he said.

"That's nice."

He had a new teacher on Monday. Justin had no idea how long she'd last, but at least he finally knew who was being tested.

THE DUMPSTER DOLL

If I wasn't such a good runner, I'd be dead already. The whole Delbarton family was after me, just because I laughed at their little sister and made her cry. Her dress really was ugly. Somebody had to tell her the truth. I was doing her a favor. What a stupid little crybaby.

All five of the brothers—including that enormous monster, Juvie—had tried to run me down. But I was ahead of them. It was looking good. I'd cut across the vacant lot by the old movie theater, hoping I could get out of sight. I'd just turned down Clancy Street when I twisted my ankle. I went down hard.

But the pain I felt was nothing compared to what the Delbartons would do to me. I pushed myself back to my feet.

Man. Bad move. Real pain shot through my ankle. I could hear Juvie and the others less than half a block away. They'd be rounding the corner in a second. I needed to hide.

Where?

There!

A Dumpster. The lid was open. I didn't see a bunch of bags piled up in it. Perfect. I didn't mind a little garbage. I hopped over to it, grabbed the edge, hoisted myself up, and tumbled inside.

The Dumpster didn't smell like fresh garbage, but it sure didn't smell like fresh air, either. Bad smells lingered from whatever was in there earlier.

Right now, it was empty except for a brown paper bag. The bag was standing up, but it fell when I thudded into the bottom of the Dumpster.

Something tumbled out.

A doll.

A dirty, broken doll. It was a little boy with black hair and brown eyes. One arm was missing. "You're even uglier than the Delbarton girl's dress," I said.

The footsteps got closer.

I huddled in a corner, not that it would do any good if they spotted me.

The footsteps raced past. I took a deep breath. That was a mistake. I choked back a cough as the odors stabbed at my throat.

The footsteps came back.

Five Delbarton faces looked down at me. I got ready to take a pummeling. Instead of hitting me, they shut the lid.

It slammed down with a bang loud enough to make me jump. Then I heard another sound. A smaller clink. They'd flipped the latch—the one you slip a lock through. Even without a lock on it, I was afraid I wouldn't be able to lift the Dumpster's lid. I knew they were pretty heavy.

They smacked the sides a couple times. I felt like I was inside a bass drum. At least I had the pleasure of hearing one of them shout in pain when he kicked the Dumpster.

Then I heard them walk off.

I pushed against the lid, but it didn't move. I was trapped. I could feel myself starting to panic. *Calm down*, I told myself. I'd wait a couple minutes, until I was sure they were gone. Then I could bang on the side. Someone would hear it sooner or later. Or someone would lift the lid to dump garbage. Either way, I wouldn't be stuck here forever.

"Might as well make myself comfortable," I muttered. I scrunched against one corner, and stretched my legs out.

That's when I felt the sharp sting in my calf.

"Ouch!" I shouted as I yanked my leg back, pulling my knee to my chest. I felt my calf. There was a rip in my pants. Beneath the rip, the skin was tender.

Must have caught it on something, I thought. There was probably a jagged spot in the metal on the bottom. I'd have to be more careful. It would be really easy for any cut I got in this bucket of germs to become infected.

"Ouch!"

I felt a stab in the other leg. No—not a stab. A bite. That's what it felt like. My neighbor's cat likes to bite. So I know what it feels like.

I pulled both legs in.

Something scraped along the bottom of the Dumpster. It sounded like someone was slowly dragging a small bowling ball across a sidewalk. But it wasn't steady. There'd be a slow scrape; then it would stop. That would be followed by a small thunk, followed by more scraping.

I could only picture one thing that could make that series of sounds. As soon as I thought of it, I let out a scream, to drive the image away.

The doll.

I listened.

Thunk.

He stretched his one arm out ahead of himself and let it drop.

Scrape.

He pulled himself along the Dumpster, toward me.

"No!" I kicked out hard. My foot connected with something. I heard the doll smack into the far wall of the Dumpster. "I hope I shattered your stupid head!"

My pleasure died quickly as pain shot through my ankle. I'd kicked him with the wrong foot.

Thunk.

Scrape.

"Leave me alone!"

I listened, trying to tell exactly where he was. Even in the dead blackness inside the Dumpster, I could imagine what he looked like as he dragged himself along, his porcelain jaws wide open, eager to bring me more pain. This time, I was going to use my good foot.

Thunk.

Scrape.

I waited.

Thunk.

Scrape.

I kicked hard.

Again, he smacked against the other side.

It didn't stop him.

I thrust my elbow into the wall behind me. It was hard, but it flexed a bit. That's why the doll wasn't getting smashed. The wall wasn't rigid enough.

Next time, I'd raise my foot and smash my heel down on him. That would do it. I'd shatter his head.

I listened.

Nothing.

Then, faintly, I heard a different sound. Quiet. Slow.

Rolling? Was he rolling toward me, like a baby crossing a floor?

"Ow!"

I slapped at the outside of my leg as he bit me in the thigh.

My hand connected with something hard.

I screamed again as I felt a bite on my palm.

Panicked, I shot to my feet.

Or tried to.

My head slammed against the top of the Dumpster.

I crumpled to the floor, dizzy. Flashes of light spun past my eyes in the darkness. I felt like I was going to throw up. Fear and nausea joined forces in my stomach and fought to turn me into a crying, shivering, puking mess.

Amidst the pain of my head and the screaming of my brain, I felt another bite on my leg. I was ready to give up and collapse to the floor.

But there was also another flash of light. I looked up. I saw a slight gap in the side of the Dumpster where the lid met the top of the compartment. I'd slammed the top so hard with my head, I must have popped the latch up.

I can get out.

I put my hand up, stood cautiously, and pushed.

The lid raised up. It was heavy, but I managed to push it all the way over. It banged down against the outside.

Light and fresh air invaded my dungeon.

Free.

I stood. The doll bit my ankle. I kicked back, knocking him away.

All I had to do was pull myself over the edge, and I could escape him.

No. Escape wasn't good enough. I needed to destroy him first. I wanted to crush his head into a powder beneath my heel. Then I'd tear off his remaining arm, as well as his legs. Maybe I'd bring the pieces home and burn them in the backyard.

I turned to face him. "It's over," I said, looking down.

He looked up at me with painted eyes, a torn piece of my pants leg clamped in his mouth.

"Yeah, you heard me," I said. "It's over. I won."

I held on to the side of the Dumpster and raised my good foot. "How do you like it now?" I said. Maybe I'd stomp him a bit at a time, so I could extend the pleasure.

Yeah. I'd stomp on one side first. Crush his cheek. Grind his ear beneath my foot. This was going to feel so good.

"He got out!"

I spun toward the shout. The new pain in my ankle brought me to my knees.

The Delbartons raced toward the Dumpster.

"No!" I screamed as they closed the lid again, bringing back the darkness.

I banged and yelled.

"Get a stick," I heard Juvie say. "Put it through the latch."

I screamed and banged. I rammed the lid. It held. I fell to my side. I felt another bite near my knee, and then one on my hip.

I batted at the doll, but I was weak. The bites moved closer to my face. I screamed louder, hoping to mask the pain with my shouts. It didn't work. I felt every bite on my face, my shoulders, and my neck. And then, I felt nothing.

M.U.B.

"Psssttt . . ."

"Who's that?"

"You know who it is."

"No, I don't. Go away."

"Sorry. I can't do that."

"This is my room. Get out!"

"Technically, it's my room, too."

"You're not real. Go away."

"If I'm not real, who are you talking to?"

"My imagination."

"Can your imagination shake the bed?"

"Stop that!"

"It makes me sad to be told I'm not real. Sad and angry."

"All right! You're real. Stop shaking the bed."

"You sure shout a lot."

"You're scaring me."

"That's my job."

"Why?"

"It's what I'm good at."

"I don't like it."

"You can't like everything that's good for you."

"You're not good for me. You're a monster."

"I can't be both?"

"How can you be good for me?"

"Remember last week when your friends wanted you to climb that cliff and dive into the river?"

"Yeah."

"Did you do it?"

"No. Of course not."

"Why?"

"I didn't feel like it."

"Liar."

"Shut up."

"Why didn't you do it?"

"I was afraid I'd get hurt real badly."

"Have you ever been hurt real badly?"

"No."

"Then what makes you afraid of that?"

"I don't know."

"Sure you do."

"No, I don't."

"Grrrrrr!"

"Hey! Stop snarling. You're scaring me."

"What makes you afraid?"

"You do."

"So, if it weren't for me, you might have dived into that river and gotten badly hurt."

"No way."

"Way."

"No way."

"Grrrrrr!"

"Okay. Maybe."

"Thanks. It's nice to be appreciated."

"You're really here for my own good?"

"That's one way of looking at it."

"So I don't have to worry if I let my hand dangle over the side. You won't bite my fingers off?"

"I never said that. I like fingers. They're crunchy and chewy."

"Stop it. You're scaring me again."

"That's my job. Just go to sleep."

"How can I sleep when I'm scared?"

"That's another thing you'll learn."

"Just be quiet."

"Okay."

"Can I dangle my foot?"

"Not a good idea."

"You'd eat it?"

"Ick, no. Do you have any idea what sort of things you stepped in today?"

"So why can't I dangle it?"

"I'd grab it and drag you under. I can't help myself. Just keep everything up there where it belongs."

"Okay. Good night."

"Good night. Sweet dreams."

SYMPATHY PAINS

I know you're supposed to like, or even love, your blood relatives. But my cousin Chelsea is hard to like and impossible to love. That didn't used to be a problem, back when she lived halfway across the country, in Louisiana. Those days, I'd see her maybe once a year.

Last month, she and her folks came to live with us. Her dad got a new job up here, and they wanted to make sure it would last before they rented an apartment. So they're going to be at our place for at least another month or two. Chelsea's angry about it. She's angry about everything. I don't know why. She's really pretty, with dark hair that's just a bit curly at the ends, and big brown eyes with great lashes. She could be a model or something.

She has no reason to be angry. I'm the one who has to share my bedroom. I'm the one who has to spend the day in school with her. We're the same age, so she's in my grade. At least she's not in all my classes. That's part of the problem. Chelsea might not like the food or the weather in Vermont, and she might not like her classmates, and she might not like being away from all her friends, but all of that is nothing compared to how she feels about her reading teacher.

"She hates me," Chelsea said after her very first day in school, as we were walking home.

"Who hates you?" I asked.

"Mrs. Bancroft," she said. "That stupid reading teacher."

I don't think they let you teach reading if you're stupid. I didn't bother telling her what I was thinking. I'd learned that the best way to deal with Chelsea was to sound sympathetic. "That's too bad."

My sympathy didn't turn off Chelsea's ranting. She complained all the way home. "So what if I make mistakes? So what if I don't do good when I read out loud. I read just fine. I think she hates me 'cause I'm not from around here."

"That's really too bad," I said. It wasn't that I didn't care. I'd had Mrs. Bancroft last year. She wasn't my favorite teacher. She was pretty strict. But she was strict with everyone. I never got the feeling she hated any of her students.

Things got worse. Every single day, on the way home, Chelsea complained about how mean and evil her teacher was. She tried to change classes, but they wouldn't let her. She even tried to get sent to a different school. That didn't work, either. Finally, last week, she said, "I'm going to take care of this myself. She's going to be sorry she ever treated me bad."

I felt a chill, and thought about those stories I'd seen on the news where kids did something violent in school. If she was planning something like that, I'd have to stop her. "What are you talking about?"

"My friend Crystal, back home. Her mama knows dark secrets. She can hurt people. Hurt them bad. I asked Crystal to send me instructions."

"Instructions?" This was sounding worse and worse.

"For a spell," Chelsea said.

Most of the stress drained from my body. Spells didn't worry me. I believed in science and math, not spells and magic. Maybe casting some silly spells would make Chelsea feel better. That would be fine with me.

Three days later, she got a package in the mail, wrapped in brown paper. It was small. About the size of a shoe box for little-kid shoes. She hurried off with it to the attic.

I waited a couple minutes, then went up there. When I pushed open the trapdoor, Chelsea looked over her shoulder and said, "Go away."

"I'm just curious," I said. That was true.

"You can't tell anyone," she said.

"I won't." I stepped through the opening. "What's in the box?"

She held up a doll. No, it was more like a tiny mannequin. It looked like it was made of dirty wax. "Is that a voodoo doll?" I asked.

"They don't call it that," she said.

"What do you do with it?" I asked.

She put down the doll and picked up a sheet of paper covered with cramped lines of tiny handwriting. "I have instructions. I have to—" She frowned, looked at the paper for a moment, then said, "—affix it. That's what she wrote. I have to affix it to the—" She paused again to read, "—to the identity of the victim."

"Victim?" I asked.

"Victim," Chelsea said, as if the word were the sweetest ever spoken, coated with honey and cinnamon. "She'll be sorry."

I looked over Chelsea's shoulder and saw several long, thick needles in the box. I flinched at the thought of getting stuck with one of them. Chelsea went back to reading the instructions, frowning and moving her lips.

Against my better judgment, I asked, "Want me to read it to you?"

"No!" she shouted at me. "I can read just fine." She held up the wax figure. "Don't make me get another one of these."

"Good grief! I was just trying to help. Don't threaten me." I left Chelsea alone in the attic with her madness.

That evening, she almost seemed happy. She hummed as we cleared the table after dinner, and smiled as she did her homework.

The next day, I noticed Mrs. Bancroft limping in the hallway. "Are you all right?" I asked.

She smiled at me. "Oh, it's nothing. Just a little twinge of arthritis. It hurt quite a bit last night, but it's getting better pretty quickly. Thank you for asking."

At the end of the day, I saw her again, and she was barely limping.

"It's not strong enough," Chelsea said as we headed home.

"What?"

"The connection. I hurt her. But not bad. I want to make her suffer as much as she made me suffer. Then we'll be even."

She went right to the attic when we got home. I followed her. When she lifted the lid of the box, I saw a pin jabbed into the right knee of the doll. I thought back to the hallway, and pictured Mrs. Bancroft limping. Yeah, it was the right knee. I tried to convince myself it was a coincidence.

Chelsea took a pencil from her purse and placed it next to the doll. "This is hers," she said. "It will strengthen the connection."

"Are you sure she hasn't suffered enough?" I asked.

"What? Not even close!" She grabbed another of the pins and jabbed it into the doll's left shoulder.

I backed away and left the attic.

The next day, I didn't see Mrs. Bancroft in the hall, so I walked to her room. When I reached the doorway, I leaned in and asked, "How's your knee?"

"Much better." Then she rubbed her left shoulder. "I guess small pains are a part of life when you reach my age."

"Your shoulder hurts?" I asked.

She started to shrug, then flinched. "A little. But I've felt worse."

I knew who was going to feel even worse. Sure enough, on the way home, Chelsea couldn't control her anger. "That's it. I'm doing every step this time. I'm totally . . . What's that word?"

I thought back to the other day. "Associating?"

"Yeah. That's it. This was just a test. I know it works. Now I'm going to make her suffer big-time."

I wasn't sure what to do. I could tell on her, but who would believe me? I could hide the doll, but she'd get another one. I thought about it when we got home. I even went online to see if I could find out anything real about all this stuff. As I searched, I could hear her over my head, shuffling around in the attic. Twice she came downstairs for something. After a while, and after visiting dozens of weird, strange, and disturbing Web sites, I realized I was wasting my time. Anyone who really knew about this stuff wouldn't be talking about it online.

In the end, I came up with only one idea. If there were more instructions, maybe she'd have trouble with them. I could offer to help, and tell her the wrong stuff to do. I couldn't let her hurt Mrs. Bancroft anymore.

I went up to the attic.

"You're just in time," Chelsea said.

"For what?" The doll was dressed in a black skirt and blue blouse now. It was the sort of thing Mrs. Bancroft would wear. There were three tiny bracelets on her left wrist. It looked like they'd been made of scraps of wire.

"For Mrs. Bancroft to feel a whole lot of pain." Chelsea raised the needle over the doll. It looked like she was aiming right for the heart.

I had to stop her.

Maybe I could distract her by asking questions. If I got her talking, she might calm down. I pointed to the doll's head. "Is that her hair? How'd you get it?" From the little tiny bit I'd learned—or, at least, from the one thing nearly all the Web sites mentioned—spells like this worked best when you had some hair or fingernail clippings from the victim.

"It doesn't have to be hers," Chelsea said.

I looked at the hair on the doll again. It was just a bit curly. Like Chelsea's. Exactly like Chelsea's. I noticed a scissors on the floor next to the box. She must have misread the instructions and thought any hair would do. "Wait! Stop!" I reached for her wrist.

"No!" Chelsea slammed the needle into the heart of the doll.

I screamed. So did she. She stood and clutched her chest. I yanked out the needle, but it was too late. Chelsea collapsed, hitting the floor with a thud. Her eyes were open, but she wasn't seeing anything. I ran for help, but I knew it wouldn't do any good. Chelsea was gone. Hate and ignorance had killed her.

ROUGH ROAD

There was a troll under the bridge. I could see part of his huge back and one flopped-out arm, the limp fingers looking like large sausages that had been left outside to rot. Even if he'd been fully hidden, the smell would have revealed his presence. You could scrub a troll all day and all night with harsh soap, and he'd still smell like a dead animal that had been soaked in swamp water for a week and then coated with vomit.

I studied the slow rise and fall of his back. At least he was asleep. I placed one foot onto the first plank of the bridge and eased my weight down, listening for the slightest creak. Trolls were fairly sound sleepers. Their hearing isn't great. Their ears tend to be clogged with scabs, wax, and dead insects. But I didn't want to take any chances. If I woke him, I'd have to run hard and fast until he gave up the chase. Trolls don't have a lot of endurance, but running is a last option around here, at best. It's too easy to flee from one danger right into the arms, claws, or jaws of another. And there were plenty of other dangers ahead of me.

I made it across the bridge in silence. Half a mile later, I heard faint singing. It was coming from the left side of the trail, up ahead. There was a steep drop on that side. It had to be Sirens, trying to lure travelers to their death. I had wax in my backpack. I took a piece out, broke it in half, and, feeling slightly troll-like, plugged my ears.

I was pleased with my cleverness in avoiding danger until I noticed the shadow moving up from behind me. I rolled to the right side of the path just as the basilisk leaped toward me. As he came down, I kicked out hard, sending him over the side of the ridge, making sure to avert my eyes.

I realized he'd teamed up with the Sirens. That was new, and dangerous. I moved ahead, waiting until I was far out of range before removing the wax. I took a careful look around, making sure nothing else was stalking me.

When I reached the boulder pile, I took out my grappling hook and started the climb. It was a difficult way to go. But I preferred it to the road, which passed through the field of corpses. They were slow, and easy to fight, but the stench was close to unbearable, maybe even worse than that of an ogre, and the sight was fairly troubling.

There were snakes and scorpions hiding among the boulders, but my boots gave me plenty of protection, and I was careful not to put my hands down where I could be bitten. I knew from experience that even a small scorpion bite takes ages to heal, and continues to hurt even after all signs of the wound are gone.

Just one more mile, I thought when I clambered down off the last boulder and headed for the woods.

I had to hide behind a tree for several minutes after a Minotaur crashed through the path ahead of me and paused, snorting steam from his nostrils and looking around for someone to gore with his deadly horns. He dashed off soon enough.

Finally, I reached the far side of the woods. *Almost there.* I'd just stepped into the clearing when something blotted out the sun. I looked up, already knowing what I'd see.

Dragons. Lots of them.

They have a hard time spotting anything that isn't moving. I had a hard time standing still. I was tempted to dive back into the woods. But if they saw me, and they were hungry, they'd torch the entire woods to drive me out.

So I stood still and waited for them to pass.

But they didn't pass. They landed in the clearing. I was trapped until they flew off. But I couldn't stay there. I had to keep going.

I watched as they wandered through the field. There were seven of them, strolling around, sniffing the earth once in a while, as if they were on the trail of some quarry or enemy. Every once in a while, all of them would end up facing away from me. At every opportunity, I'd take a step or two, circling wide of their paths. As soon as one started to turn toward me, I'd freeze.

It took forever, but I finally reached the other side of a low crest. Once I was sure I was out of their sight, I ran toward the small wooden building. I reached the door and hurried through.

"William, you're late," Miss Everlearn said.

"There were dragons," I said. "Seven of them."

"No excuses," she said. "Be grateful you have a school here. We've already started the math lesson. Take out your textbook and turn to page forty-seven."

"Yes, ma'am." I took my book from my backpack and followed along with the lesson. After math, it was time for language arts. We were reading a story about a boy and girl who lived in a world where it was safe and easy to walk to school. A world without ogres, Sirens, basilisks, and walking corpses. I enjoyed it a lot. I love fantasy.

NO THANKS

You need to write thank-you notes," Edwina's mom said, handing her a box of cards.

"I will, Mom," Edwina said. But she wouldn't. It was a lie—the same lie she'd told every birthday and Christmas since she'd been old enough to write. Unbeknownst to Edwina, who didn't keep track of such things, she'd just received her 128th never-to-be-thanked-for present and was about to not send her 128th note. The number 128 might not seem special to you or to me, and it would definitely not seem special to Edwina, but it did mean a lot to the universe. The universe likes order. Two times two is four. Two times four is eight. Keep going, and you hit 128.

Edwina stuck the thank-you notes behind her dresser with all the others. It was getting crowded back there. The ingratitude caused a rumbling in the cosmos. Edwina's aunt, Tish, living just across the street, was the first to arrive. She rang the front bell, said hello to her sister (Edwina's mother), who let her in, then walked up to Edwina's room, scooped up everything she had given her niece, turned away, and left the room without a word.

Edwina's uncle Alvin, who lived across town, showed up next. Edwina's parents' friends, who had been nice enough to give her presents, came after that. Eventually, Edwina's room was nearly stripped bare.

All that remained was a scattering of presents from her grandparents. She hadn't gotten anything from them for the last three years. They were dead.

Edwina wasn't smart enough to figure out why the doorbell rang again. She did start to get an idea what was happening when she heard her mother scream. She got an even better idea when her dad joined the screaming. Her dad never screamed.

The idea became totally solid and inescapable when she heard the slow footsteps in the hallway outside her bedroom.

It was not a pleasant reunion.

Edwina tried to stop screaming after her grandparents left, but she didn't seem to be able to control her lungs or her throat for quite a while.

When she finally stopped screaming, and was able to actually think in words again, her first thought was, *I'm sending cards from now on.*

That would be easy enough for her to do. She had quite a supply of thank-you cards behind her dresser, and she probably wouldn't be receiving many presents in the near future.

COFFIN FITS

There's this kid I know, Felix Bartholemieux. He's sort of my friend, but he played the meanest trick ever on me last week. I need to get him back. And I know just how I'll do it.

I guess I should explain the trick. Felix's parents own a funeral home. Felix invited me over last week. His house is next door to the funeral parlor.

"I'll show you something really cool," he said right after I got there.

I followed him out of the house, toward the funeral parlor. "It's not a body, is it?" I definitely didn't want to see a dead person.

"Relax. It's nothing like that."

He went through a side door, leading me into a room with a bunch of coffins in it. But I wasn't scared, because they were all open and empty. I guess it was sort of a showroom for display models. Felix didn't stop there. He led me into a second room. This one was dark, and the coffins were closed.

"Are there people in them?" I asked, getting ready to make

a dash for the door. I'm not a coward, but that sort of stuff just creeped me out.

Felix laughed. "Don't be silly. This is where my parents keeps the extra ones." He walked over to the closest coffin and lifted the lid. "Most people never get to find out what it feels like inside. But I climb in them all the time. Try it. It's like sitting in a luxury car."

I didn't want to get in trouble with his parents. "You sure it's okay?"

"Totally. Just take your shoes off."

So I kicked off my shoes, climbed in, lay down, and crossed my arms on my chest, like I see them do with dead people in the movies. I looked over toward Felix, but he wasn't there.

"Good night!" Felix said from the other side. He slammed the lid down. It got really dark. I heard some sort of latch slide in place.

"Hey!" I banged on the lid. Then I pushed on it. It didn't move. I wasn't afraid of small spaces. And I wasn't afraid of the dark. But I guess I was pretty much terrified by small, dark spaces.

Stay calm, I told myself.

That didn't work. I started to scream, and I kept banging and kicking. It was hard to make much noise—the inside was all padded. It was like punching a thin mattress. Finally, Felix slid back the latches and lifted the lid. I climbed out, ready to punch him in the face.

But he grabbed my arms and said, "What's wrong? Can't you take a joke?"

"That wasn't funny," I said as I tried to decide whether to hit him in the nose or the jaw. If I broke his nose, I'd get in big trouble, but it would be worth it.

"Sure it was. It was hilarious," he said. "And you're the first person I've done it to, because I think you're the coolest kid in our class. I knew you could take a joke. But here's the best part—now we can do it to everyone else. One at a time. It will be awesome. And you'll be in on it from the start. You'll be my prank partner. Isn't that great?"

I paused a second, to make it look like I was thinking this over. But I'd already thought about it, and I'd made a decision. I'd pretend to go along with Felix until I had a chance to get even. Finally, I nodded and said, "Wow. That's pretty cool." I was going to add, *Thanks for picking me first.* But I didn't want to risk sounding too enthusiastic right away.

Anyhow, all of that happened last week. This morning, Felix told me he'd picked his next victim. It was Lawrence Mott. It really didn't matter who he picked, because it was Felix who was going to be the victim. I was ready to get him back, big-time.

"We'll head to my house right after school," he said.

"Can it wait until tomorrow?" I asked.

"Nope," Felix said. "I already invited him over. It has to be today."

Great. I figured he'd say that. He was falling right into my trap. I'd given all of this a ton of thought. I'd actually thought about nothing else all week. I'd had plenty of time to work out the perfect plan. "Oh, man. I can't come today. I have a dentist's appointment after school."

Felix shrugged. "There'll be plenty more chances." He didn't seem to care that I was missing the prank.

After school, I hurried over to the funeral parlor. I sneaked in through the side door and found the coffin Felix had trapped me in. I figured he'd use the same one this time that he'd used to scare me. But when he opened the lid, he'd be in for a surprise. I'd leap up and scream. That would scare him so bad, I'd bet he'd need to change his pants.

I wasn't scared at all this time, since I knew I could get out whenever I wanted. Of course, I wanted to get out right in Felix's face. And I would. I climbed into the coffin, lowered the lid, and waited.

It's hard to tell how much time has passed when you're in the dark. But after a while—maybe five minutes—I heard footsteps and voices. It was pretty muffled inside the coffin. I decided it would be even more awesome if I didn't jump out right away. I'd cross my hands on my chest and close my eyes, so I'd look dead. That would startle Felix. And then he'd be even more scared when I let out a terrifying scream and leaped to life. He'd get scared twice. This was so perfect. Felix was going to regret that he'd ever played a trick on me.

Muffled voices moved closer to the coffin. I allowed myself a quick grin before I forced my face to look dead. A smile would give away the joke.

Light hit my eyelids as Felix raised the coffin lid. I opened my eyes the tiniest slit, so I could see Felix's expression when he noticed me.

But I didn't see Felix.

I saw something huge, right over me. It was somebody's back. But it was enormous. There were hands on his shoulders, and other hands on his feet. He was so big, whoever was carrying him couldn't even see around him.

Before I could sit up, they dropped him on me. It was like getting hit with a dolphin. The body smashed me flat and knocked the wind out of my lungs. I couldn't even turn my head sideways to catch my breath.

"Phew, that was rough," someone said.

"He's bigger than I realized," a second voice said. "Help me push him down a bit."

The body got pressed down even harder. I was afraid I'd burst. I heard the lid slam. My hands were trapped at my sides. I was getting dizzy. I struggled with all my strength and managed to turn my head sideways enough so I could breathe.

"Help!" I yelled. The sound was swallowed by the enormous body on top of me. I tried to kick at the sides of the coffin. It was no use. I was pinned flat. I couldn't move my legs at all.

I had to get out. If I didn't, they'd never find me. I'd be one of those missing kids you see on the news. Wild ideas flashed through my mind. I wondered if I could chew my way through the body. The thought almost made me throw up. I choked back my nausea. If I puked, I'd be dead for sure. There had to be another way out.

Think!

Nothing. There was no other choice. There was a movie about a guy who cut his own arm off when he was trapped climbing a mountain. At least this wouldn't be my own arm.

I turned my head, opened my mouth, fought back against my churning stomach with every ounce of willpower I had, and chomped down.

"Owwwwwwcch!"

The scream came from right over my head. It was followed by a shift in pressure as the body flung open the coffin lid and sat up. It tumbled out, leaving me stunned, numb, and trembling.

I blinked against the bright lights overhead. The scream had shifted to smaller cries of pain, which were drowned out by laughter.

I sat up.

Five kids were in the room. Felix and three other kids from my class were looking at me and howling with laughter. The fifth kid, Augie Durback, the biggest kid in our class, was holding his shoulder and glaring at me.

"You bit me," Augie said. He rubbed his shoulder.

"I . . ." There were no words. I slumped back in the coffin. My perfect prank had been turned around, and I'd been turned into a fool. They might as well bury me now. Once this story spread around the school, my life would be over.

Felix peered at me from the side of the coffin. "Hey, man. Cheer up. You can help us get the next one. It will be awesome."

Yeah. Right. Sure. Awesome. It would be great to pull off a joke on someone else. But I had a funny feeling it just wouldn't work out as planned.

WALNUTS

"We're getting a new student," Mrs. Persham said. "He'll be here soon. But we need to talk first."

"I wonder what's wrong with him?" I whispered to Matty, who was sitting next to me.

"Nothing that's not wrong with you, Jasper," Matty said.

I punched him. He punched me back. Mrs. Persham glared at us until we sat up in our seats and pretended to pay attention.

"Little Dwight has a walnut allergy," she said.

"No nuts?" Cindy Washinski asked.

"That stinks," I said. There were three classrooms where you couldn't have any kind of food, just in case there were nuts in it.

"Just walnuts," Mrs. Persham said. "Don't be so selfish, Jasper. It won't be a big deal."

And it wouldn't have been, if Dwight had been a normal kid. But he was totally freaked out about the possibility of ever coming close to a walnut. Before he came into our classroom for the first time, he peeked his head in the door, sniffed, stared all around like he had some sort of X-ray vision, then looked over at Mrs. Persham and asked, "Has the room been checked?"

"It's totally safe," she said. She smiled. But even her good nature faded by the second week. Dwight didn't relax for a moment. If someone opened a window in the classroom, he scurried over to make sure there was nothing dangerous outside. That was totally ridiculous, since we were on the second floor. If someone brought a package into the room, he'd leap from his desk, flee to the back of the room, and shout, "Check it!"

So, yeah, we were all getting a bit tired of the routine. Which is why I finally decided I'd had enough and brought a bag of walnuts to school in my backpack.

I got there early and slipped the bag into my desk. When Dwight came in, I watched him, to see if he started to turn red or swell up. But he looked fine.

He sat two rows over from me. After he took his seat, I opened my desk and took out a walnut. Then I waited for the bell to ring. Under cover of the noise, I rolled the walnut toward him, aiming it so it would stop under his chair.

Perfect.

It stopped exactly where I wanted, right under him.

He seemed fine.

That did it. I decided I'd expose him, and get our class back to normal.

"Faker!" I said. I grabbed the bag, stood up, and pointed under his seat.

He looked down, then screamed and stood on his chair.

"You aren't allergic." I opened the bag and walked toward him. "Admit it."

"I'm not allergic to walnuts!" he shouted.

"I knew it." I flung the open bag at him.

"They're allergic to me!"

What?

As I tried to make sense of that, something even more puzzling happened. The walnuts I'd flung stuck to his body. They started to swell. The hard shells shattered. Creatures like swollen hermit crabs burst out.

Dwight got the worst of it. They ripped into him. But as soon as he fell, they swarmed all over the room. I ran for the door, but someone bumped into me and I fell.

I felt something stinging my ankles, and then my legs. I tried to push myself to my feet, but I felt weak and dizzy. I couldn't breathe. Whatever was in their bites, I was badly allergic to it. Very badly.

A LITTER BIT OF TROUBLE

Did you change the cat litter yet, Samantha?" Mom asked when I came in from shooting baskets in the driveway.

"I was just about to," I said. I didn't mind most of my chores. Setting the table wasn't a problem. Dragging the garbage cans out to the curb wasn't too bad. Taking care of the recycling was sort of fun—I liked crushing the aluminum cans. And I liked helping with the ironing. But cat litter—yuck. I always put it off as long as I could.

I went down the hall to the laundry room to see if the litter really needed to be changed. That's where we kept the box. I wished Muffins and Boots could go outside. But our last two cats had both been hit by cars—so Muffins and Boots got to be indoor cats. Don't blame me for the names, by the way. Mom came up with them.

I was right by the doorway to the laundry room, looking at the assorted lumps lurking beneath the surface of the litter, when the doorbell rang. "I'll get it," I called.

It was my friend Treena, holding her soccer ball. "Want to kick the ball around?" she asked.

"Sure." Saved from the litter—at least for the moment. "I'm going outside with Treena for fresh air and exercise," I said as I raced out the door. That was the sort of phrase Mom would use, and the sort of thing she would urge me to do if she thought I was watching too much TV. So she could hardly argue, or tell me to stay inside.

Treena and I played until it started to grow dark. When I got home, I expected Mom to immediately ask me about the litter. Instead, she smiled, went to the fridge, grabbed the pitcher, and poured a big glass of fresh-squeezed lemonade—the kind she makes with a special homemade sugar syrup.

"Here you go, Samantha."

"Thanks," I said as she handed me the glass.

Wow—she seemed happy. I sipped the lemonade and wandered down the hall. When I reached the laundry room, I saw a perfectly smooth, flat layer of litter in the box. I guess whatever she was happy about, it had made her want to give me a break and empty the litter box herself.

That deserved a hug. I went back to the kitchen, put my glass down, and gave Mom a real hug—not the kind I get from my cousins at family reunions, but the kind I give my friends when they share really wonderful news.

"Well, you're in a good mood," Mom said.

"So are you."

We stared at each other for a moment; then we both laughed. Two days later, Mom started to ask me about emptying the litter again. I guess that was fair, since I couldn't expect her to do one of my chores for me all the time.

But I got distracted that afternoon when my friend Alicia called to ask me if I wanted to help her find a nice dress to wear to her uncle's wedding. And the next day, my aunt had tickets to take me to a concert. The day after that, the litter box was looking pretty full, and Muffin and Boots were giving me impatient stares. But I needed to go to the corner store to look at magazines. I promised myself I'd take care of the litter as soon as I got back from town.

Once again, the box was clean when I got home. And once again, Mom was especially nice to me afterwards. Whatever was making her happy, I hoped it never stopped.

I was starting to like this new arrangement. It seemed that all I had to do was hold off for an extra day or two, and Mom would decide to do me a favor. But it worked out for her, too. She got lots of hugs. And I was so happy about not having to clean the litter that I did all my other chores cheerfully.

Everything was perfect until this afternoon. The box had been really full when I went out to the mall. When I got home, I thought all the clumps were gone, but a motion caught my eye. One tiny clump of litter was in the corner. As I thought about whether I should get rid of it, the clump rolled up the side of the litter box.

I watched, unable to make sense of what I was seeing. It fell over the side and hit the floor, breaking into three smaller clumps. All the clumps rolled slowly toward the wall. They also rolled closer together, and formed back into a single clump.

The clump rolled over to the hole where the dryer vent goes. I saw it slip behind the wall. Then I heard it slowly rolling up the inside of the wall. When it got to the top, it rolled onto the ceiling.

"What in the world—?" I whispered as I looked up. I thought about all that litter, gathering above the ceiling. Weeks and weeks' worth of clumps might be up there, over my head.

That's got to be heavy.

The thought came several seconds too late to save me. I heard a creak and a crack. Something broke through the plasterboard ceiling and fell down. It crashed into my shoulder, knocking me to the floor.

A terrible weight pressed down on me for an instant, pounds and pounds of litter, nearly knocking me out with an overpowering smell of ammonia and other things too horrible to mention. And then, it rose. The clumped litter, looking like a crudely formed and nauseating three-foot-tall gingerbread man, stood up, stepped away from me, and headed down the hall, leaving behind a crunchy trail of small bits and foul clumps.

My shoulder ached. I flexed it. It wasn't broken, but I had a feeling I'd have one monster of a bruise.

I heard a scream. Then I heard the front door open.

I walked into the hall and checked out the carpet. It was looking pretty crunchy, with all those bits of litter strewn across it.

Mom appeared at the other end of the hallway. She looked pretty pale. I had a feeling I did, too. We stared at each other for a moment.

"You're cleaning this up," she said.

"I know."

"And you're scooping the litter every day."

"I know."

"Every single day."

I nodded. She walked away.

I went to get the broom.

Right after I started to sweep up the laundry room floor, Boots jumped into the clean litter box. She did her business, kicked some litter over the clump, and walked off.

I grabbed the scooper. From now on, I was going to make sure the litter box wasn't just cleaned every day—I was going to clean it as soon as it got dirty. Every single time.

The doorbell rang. I went to see who it was.

"Soccer?" Treena asked.

"Okay." I headed out. But I promised myself I'd take care of the litter as soon as I got home. For sure.

MOVING STAIRS

They were heading toward Florida to visit the grandparents. The afternoon of the second day, Dale's parents pulled off the highway to look for lunch.

"Nice town," Dale's mom said as they drove into Lamford.

"Look at that," Dale's dad said, pointing across the town square. "Big store."

Dale looked. It was the tallest building in town, as far as he could see. On the front, above four large glass double doors, were the words: HUFFDIBLE'S. Below that, in smaller letters, it read: MEETING ALL YOUR NEEDS SINCE 1932.

"Let's go there," Dale's mom said. "I forgot to pack enough shirts."

Dale's dad sighed, but didn't argue. He parked the car across the street, popped some coins in the meter, and led the family toward Huffdible's. Dale sighed, too. He hated shopping with his parents. And he knew this wouldn't be a quick trip. His mom would take forever picking out shirts, and then she'd remember she needed something else. Meanwhile, his dad would get all involved with a display of tools, or shoes, or something else just as uninteresting.

He followed his parents inside. The store was just like any other large store he'd ever been in. There was an escalator in the center, with a directory over it. Women's shirts were on the second floor. Dale didn't care about that. But he saw something that caught his attention. SIXTH FLOOR: TOYS, GAMES, AND MODELS.

That was worth a look. "Hey, Dad," he said as they reached the second floor, "want to go check out the models? Maybe they have some cool rocket ships. Or a Corvette . . ."

His dad started to nod. Dale could see the word *sure* forming on his lips. But in mid nod, his dad's head turned to the right. Dale sighed again as he watched his dad's eyes lock on to something.

"Gosh—they have those new wallets—the ones with the extra section for credit cards. I have to check that out."

"But . . ." Dale watched him go. Now he had a choice. He could stay with his mom. Or he could tag along after his dad.

Or he could break free.

"I'm going up to the sixth floor. I'll meet you back here in ten minutes," he told his mom. But he told it to her as quietly as he could. "Okay?" he said, louder.

She was distracted enough by the task of figuring out the final price of a blouse that was on the 5 percent off rack but with an additional 8 percent discount and a buy-two get-one-at-half-price special offer, that she nodded and said, "Sure."

Dale headed up the escalator. The floors weren't numbered. But he counted four flights, then stepped off. "Weird," he said, looking around. All he saw was luggage. But there were more floors above him. *Must have miscounted,* he thought. He went higher. Several floors later, he saw the unmistakable colors and shapes of a toy section.

He walked past the infant toys, and the play sets. The fun stuff was beyond that. He checked out the slot car sets and RC planes. Then he looked for the models. They had a couple of nice kits. *I have to bring Dad up here,* he thought. There was a good chance he could talk his father into buying him the Harley-Davidson Motorcycle Kit, or maybe even the *Millennium Falcon*. That would make the visit to his grandparents even more fun.

Dale walked back to the escalator and headed down. "I guess I need to go down six floors," he said. He wasn't worried. He'd just look for the women's shirts.

He saw men's pants and dinnerware. But no women's shirts. He kept going. "No problem," he said, speaking out loud. "I'll just go to the first floor, and then go back up one."

After going down several more levels, he stepped off. Children's clothing. That's all he saw. *I'll just ask someone.*

He looked around. There weren't any other people in sight—not in the aisles, and not at the registers. He headed back up. He figured if he could find the toys again, he could count his way down more carefully.

He got off when he saw shelves of board games. But this was a different floor from the one with the toys.

He looked at the escalator. *Up or down?*

"It doesn't matter," he said. "It doesn't matter at all."

He was right.

MATTERS OF FAX

I almost managed to get out of the house before Dad snagged me. The guys were waiting for me at the field. When it comes to escaping Dad, *almost* isn't anywhere near good enough. I had my glove in one hand and was turning the doorknob with the other, when Dad walked up behind me. "Hold on, Charles. I need some help."

"But the guys are waiting," I said.

"This won't take long. I have a ton of work, and I'll never get it done without some assistance."

He headed toward his office. I wanted to argue, but it was no use. Dad has his own business. He works at home. Once in a while, he snags me to help. If I try to argue, he'll just tell me a long story about how he worked every day after school in Grandpa's hardware store when he was a kid. It's usually quicker to just do what he wants.

"Fax these," he said, handing me a stack of papers.

"Then can I go out?" I asked.

"Sure."

"You know, most people use e-mail these days," I said.

"Faxing is almost prehistoric. Can't you just scan these and send a JPEG?"

"I've upgraded my technology," Dad said. "This fax is the latest model."

I took the papers and went over to the table at the back of Dad's office. There was a fax machine plugged into the outlet by the wall. But it wasn't the old one. I guess Dad really had upgraded his equipment, leaping all the way from prehistoric to ancient.

"Hey, Dad. I don't know how to use this one." Maybe he'd let me go if he realized it would take longer for him to teach me how to do it than to do it himself. It was worth a shot.

"They're all pretty much the same," he said. "Stop complaining and get to work. You know, when I was your age . . ."

I tuned him out and entered the phone number that was written on the cover page. Then I put the papers in the machine and hit the SEND button. After the fax dialed out, the papers started to feed through the machine, one sheet at a time. I noticed they weren't straight. I reached out to fix them. That's when my sleeve got caught.

"Hey!" I yanked at it, but the machine wouldn't let go. I yanked harder. It pulled me down. I stabbed at random buttons, hoping one of them would stop the machine.

"Help! It's eating me!" I shouted.

"Very funny," Dad muttered. He didn't even turn around to look.

"I mean it," I said. "I'm being swallowed."

"Ha-ha. That reminds me of the time my dad—your grandfather—let me use the key-making machine all by myself for the first time. . . ."

He still didn't look. My wrist was getting pulled into the

machine. I reached out with my other hand for the plug. But I lost my balance and fell forward. My whole arm went into the fax. I expected it to hurt. But it just sort of tingled.

The machine pulled the rest of me in. I felt like I was swimming through ginger ale. I stopped struggling to get free. It was no use.

I went all the way through the machine, and came out the bottom. I ended up on the floor, surrounded by the pages Dad had given me.

The machine beeped. I looked at the display. It read, FIFTEEN PAGES SENT. ONE OBJECT SENT.

One object? I tried to stand, but I was dizzy. I felt like I'd been spun around real fast about fifty times. I waited a moment, until I was sure I wouldn't topple over, then got to my feet.

One object. I couldn't get that thought out of my mind. I looked at the first page. The fax had been sent to Sebold Engineering Corp. I knew the place. I'd gone there with Dad a couple times when he dropped stuff off. It was on the other side of Broad Street, not far from here. I figured I'd better get over there and see what sort of object came out of their fax machine.

"Am I finished?" I asked Dad.

"You're done. Thanks. Go play."

I headed out. When I got right down the street from the Sebold building, I saw the front door open. Then I watched myself wander out. I ran up to me and took a good look. It was me, all right. But not as sharp as I looked in the real world. It was sort of like a slightly fuzzy version of myself.

"Hi," my other me said. He smiled at me like I was his best friend.

"Hi." I wasn't sure what to say. I wanted to be nice to him, because he was me. I certainly didn't want to be mean to my-self. But I wasn't sure I wanted another me around.

Then I realized it might work out okay. I could get my other me to go to school in my place. I'm pretty sure my teachers wouldn't notice a bit of fuzziness. And I'd always have some-one to play two-player video games with me. My folks don't let me go online, so local co-op is my only choice if I want to play with someone. I owned two controllers, even though most of my friends were usually too busy playing online to come over.

"Let's go home," I said. There was no way I could hide this from my parents. I figured I'd break it to Dad first. He was less likely to freak out than Mom. "Do you like *Gears of War*?"

"Sure. Just as much as you do."

Of course he did. He liked what I liked. This would be bet-ter than having a best friend. This would be someone who to-tally understood me. He'd know what I was thinking, and what I wanted. "Wait here," I told me when we got to the yard.

I wanted to warn Dad first, and get him ready for what he was about to see.

He was on the phone in the office. "I'm sorry. He did it by mistake," he said. "It's a new machine." Then he hung up.

"Uh, Dad . . . ," I said as the phone rang again.

He looked up at me. "I've been getting calls ever since you left. You must have hit the broadcast button."

"Broadcast?" I remembered punching all those buttons when I was getting sucked in. "What does it do?"

"It sends a fax to everyone."

I got the same feeling in my stomach that I got in school when I realized I'd forgotten to do my homework. "What do you mean, *everyone*?"

"Everyone," he said. "Every person in my contact list. The people who've called already are babbling some kind of nonsense about having you show up with the fax. I don't understand what that part is about."

"You will . . . ," I said as I glanced out the side window. I could see me coming toward the house. Lots of me. They—I mean, we—were all coming here. I guess I was going to need to get a lot more controllers.

CASTING MAGIC

I love opening day. It's the only time all year when I don't mind getting up early. You can't start fishing until 7 A.M., but if you want a good spot, you have to get out to the stream by 5. So I was awake by four, and had met up with my friends Mikey, Brian, Xavier, and Drew in front of the middle school at 4:30. The school's on the way to McLean's Creek, so it was a good spot for us to meet.

"It's freezing," Mikey said.

He's always complaining. But he was right—it was cold. I didn't mind. The crisp air made the sky awesome. The stars looked like tiny white lasers aiming at us.

"Anyone want to make a bet on who limits out first?" Brian asked.

"Why bother?" Xavier said. "You know I'll win."

That was probably true. We were all pretty good, but Xavier was the best. He had a lot more patience than I did. Most of the time, I'd cast into a spot once or twice, and then move on. But Xavier would work a spot for as long as it took. I'd seen him spend twenty minutes fishing a small riffle that the rest of us had passed by, and end up with a nice catch.

"Yeah, Xavier has all the luck," Mikey said.

"Not this year," Brian said. "So, who wants to bet?"

"Bet what?" I asked.

"The three losers do all the winner's yard work for a month," Brian said.

"I'm in," I said. It was worth a shot. We each had to mow our own lawn. Xavier's mom had a huge garden, so there wasn't a lot of grass to mow. My yard was pretty big, with lots of trees to mow around, so if I won, it would be great. Not that I had much hope.

"Me, too," Mikey said. His yard was as big as mine, but it didn't have any trees, so it was pretty easy to mow.

"What about you?" Brian asked Xavier. "Are you in or are you scared?"

Sometimes we played cards. Right now, Brian reminded me of a kid who was holding a handful of aces and trying not to act too excited. I had no idea what his secret was, but we'd find out soon enough. His yard was small, but it had a steep slope in the back that was a killer to mow.

Xavier nodded. "Sure. I'm in."

We got on our bikes and headed for the creek. There were already a lot of people along the banks, but we managed to grab one of our favorite stretches, right in casting distance of some nice rocky riffles and a deep pool we called the "mine hole." I'd pulled a nine-inch brook trout out of there last fall.

By the time we got close to seven, there were people almost elbow to elbow all along both banks. The funny thing is, it wouldn't be like this tomorrow. People made a big deal out of opening day. I guess I did, too. But half of them wouldn't even fish again this year. I fish all year long. So does Xavier.

I got my tackle ready. Normally, I liked using spinners and spoons. Especially this small one that looked like a minnow. It was called a Phoebe. But in this tight a crowd, I figured it was better to start out with live bait. I could cast that out and let it drift, or add a bit of split shot to the line and let it sit.

Xavier, to my right, was using a tiny clear float and a dry fly. "Trying something new," he said.

I glanced over at Brian, on my left, as he unscrewed the lid on a small jar like the ones that hold salmon eggs. The label looked like it was hand printed with a black fine-tipped marker. It read: MAGIC BAIT. CATCH A FISH ON EVERY CAST.

"Are you kidding?" I asked.

Brian grinned. "I found it on the Internet. It's guaranteed. It cost me two weeks' allowance, but it will be worth it when you guys mow my lawn all month. Did you know we're moving across town? The new place has a gigantic lawn on a real steep hill."

Before I could answer, I saw a flurry of motion around me and heard a dozen plops and splashes. Then I checked my watch. It was 6:59. Some people just couldn't wait. Once one person started fishing, most people joined in. I waited until 7:00. So did Xavier. I think it's important to follow the rules.

At 7:00, I flipped my worm toward the mine hole with an underhand cast. Xavier tossed his float toward the riffles and let it drift. Five seconds later, I saw the float go under as a trout hit the fly. At the same time, I saw Brian set his hook.

"Got one," Brian said.

He and Xavier each landed their first fish.

"Too small," Xavier said. You could only keep fish that

were at least six inches long. Xavier gently removed the hook. That was easy, since he'd flattened the barb.

Brian's fish was a keeper. He didn't bother to measure it, but I could tell it was at least eight inches.

I felt a tap on my line. I pulled back to set the hook, but missed the fish. I reeled in my line to check my bait. Yeah, the worm was gone. As I baited my hook, I glanced to both sides. Drew was releasing an undersize fish. Mikey hadn't caught anything yet.

"Got another!" Brian said.

He played his second fish in. That took a while, since it was a big one.

"Wow, that's got to be over a foot," I said.

"Yeah, and that's two for me," Brian put the fish in his creel bag. Then he lifted up the jar of bait and gave it a kiss. "I wonder what I should do while you guys are mowing my lawn? Maybe I'll go fishing. Or maybe I'll sit on my porch, drink lemonade, and read comic books while you sweat."

He baited his hook with another glob of his magic goop, tossed out his line, and caught another fish. At least this one was undersized.

But, the way things were going, it looked like he was right. We'd be mowing his lawn—his new, gigantic lawn. And it looked like the label on the bait spoke the truth—he was catching a fish on every cast. Not every trout was a keeper, and not every fish was a trout. He caught a couple bluegills and a perch after the trout. But he was definitely getting way ahead of us in the race to limit out.

By the time I caught my first keeper—a nice nine-inch palomino—Brian had three trout in his creel. Xavier had two. Drew had one, and Mikey was still getting skunked and complaining about what a terrible spot we'd chosen.

I tried to concentrate on my own fishing, but I realized people along the bank had started to notice the action happening next to me. Fishermen are like that. No matter what we're doing, we always check out anything that's caught by anyone else. We want to see what's in the water. And to tell the truth, we want to see if their fish is smaller. Fishing gets a lot more competitive than it should. But I guess that's true about a lot of things.

The opening-day limit was six fish. When Brian caught his fourth, I noticed a couple people had stopped fishing and moved behind us to watch him.

After landing two small trout and three more bluegills, Brian caught his fifth keeper. "Admit it," he said. "I'm the best."

There was almost no room to move now. Half the people on the stream had become spectators. One of them became a bit more than that. Nobody saw who did it, but someone gave Brian a push right when he was about to cast.

He tumbled off the bank into the creek. It wasn't deep where he fell, and it wasn't fast, but it was cold.

He let out a scream as he scrambled back onto the bank. I would have loved to capture that on video. He'd be at my mercy for the rest of his life. People spread out to give him room to scramble back onto the bank. He grabbed his tackle box and creel bag, and raced for his bike. I figured he was eager to get somewhere warm.

Everyone else went back to fishing. It felt like some sort of invisible tension had evaporated from the air. I looked down.

Brian had left his jar of magic bait behind. I picked it up and slipped it into a side pocket on my fishing vest.

After the water settled down from Brian's belly flop, Xavier caught his third fish. I still had just one. I touched the jar in my pocket. I could use it, and win. But there was no way I'd do that. I wasn't afraid of getting knocked into the water. I was smart enough to know it was a bad idea to use it on every cast and get a bunch of attention. But that's not what stopped me. It was the magic that stopped me.

Catching a fish whenever I wanted, without any need for skill or even luck? No thanks. That would take all the magic out of fishing.

SWIM SAFETY

Karlie licked the last bits of peanut butter from the side of her thumb, then hopped off the blanket where she'd been sitting while she ate her sandwich.

"Where are you going?" her mom asked.

She pointed at the ocean. "Swimming." *Where else would I be going?*

"You just ate," her mom said.

"So?"

"You'll get cramps," her dad said.

"No, I won't. That's a myth or something," Karlie said. "We learned all about it in health class." Or maybe she'd read it on the Internet or in one of her magazines. She couldn't remember for sure.

"It's better to be safe," her mom said.

"It's better not to miss out on fun," Karlie said. "Come on. Nothing will happen." She looked at the surf, where dozens of kids, bobbing in the waves, were playing, laughing, screaming, and having a lot more fun than she was. She knew some of them must have just eaten. And they all seemed fine.

"Look at that!" she yelled to her parents. "That boy's eating a hot dog. And he's in the water."

She couldn't believe someone would do that. But if it helped her get what she wanted, she was happy to point it out.

Her mom opened her mouth, like she was going to keep arguing, but then she sighed and said, "All right. Just be careful. And don't go too far out."

"I won't." Karlie raced for the water before her parents could change their minds. She waded past the boy with the hot dog, who had mustard smeared on his chin, and the other boys and girls who were playing near shore. The water stayed shallow for a long way, so she could go far past them.

As the water lapped above her belly, she noticed a blob of peanut butter on the side of her bathing suit. She wiped it off, then rubbed her fingers in the water.

I don't think sharks eat peanut butter, she thought. She wasn't worried. There weren't any sharks near this beach.

But something moved in the water. Karlie froze and tried to figure out what it was.

"Ewww . . . ," she said when she realized it was a small jellyfish. The transparent creature was barely visible, more a suggestion than a reality. Karlie stepped away from it. "Okay—one jellyfish isn't a big deal," she said.

But it wasn't just one. More showed up, clustering near the first one. And then, as Karlie backed farther away, even more drifted toward her. She spun around and saw she was surrounded. The sea on all sides of her was filled with jellyfish.

They closed in on her. The thought of touching them made her gag. But she had to get to shore. She tried to wade through them. They clung to her. She realized she was lucky they weren't the kind that stung. As the water lapped at her, they rose, clinging higher and higher on her bathing suit. They were up to her shoulders now. She was covered with jellyfish.

The weight pulled at her. She opened her mouth to scream, but something flowed into it, stifling her scream before it could emerge from her throat. It had a familiar and unexpected flavor. As her face got closer to the water, she noticed that the jellyfish surrounding her weren't totally transparent. They had a tinge of color. They were light purple, like they were made of grape jelly.

The peanut butter, she thought as the weight of the jellyfish pulled her beneath the surface of the water. That's what had attracted them.

Karlie realized her parents were right: It was dangerous to swim after eating.

DRAWN THAT WAY

"You need to slay your own demons."

That's what my art teacher always used to say. I took lessons from him for three years. Mostly pencil drawing, because that's what I like the best, but also a bit of acrylic painting and some pen-and-ink. Then, one day, he packed up his stuff and left town. I guess he had his own demons to deal with.

I suppose the saying could mean a lot of different things. I think it meant you had to solve your own problems, or maybe deal with the stuff that really scared you and held you back. Until recently, I didn't think about it all that much. But then, about a month ago, I started having bad dreams. I'd see this creature walking down a dark road, miles away from my house, sort of like I was seeing him through binoculars. Even far off, as soon as my eyes focused on him, he could tell I was watching. And when he knew he had my attention, he'd whisper, "I'm coming for you."

I'm coming for you.

The words froze my blood.

He's large. It's hard to tell for sure, since there are no people in the scene. Based on the way he looks against the road, he's at least seven feet tall. However tall he is, he's definitely strong. His muscles look like thick ropes beneath his skin.

Darkness robs color. You can't tell cobalt blue from royal purple at night, not even in dreams. But the tones that splash across his body seem, in the moonlight, to suggest shades leaning more toward red than green. It's a dull red, like old, spilled blood. His eyes aren't dull. They glow with pits of yellow fire that surround deep black pupils. His nose is a gash that looks like it was dug from his face with a pickax.

His claws are jet black, too. As are his teeth.

When I wake from each nightmare, frozen in terror, I can see that the time is always around 2 A.M.

At first, I assumed the dreams would go away. I've had my share of bad dreams. Even had some that shocked me awake, sweat drenched and screaming. Each of those nightmarish incidents had happened only once. These dreams were different. They're as steady and dependable as the sunset. Only one thing changed from dream to dream. Each night, he got closer.

At first, the background could have been anywhere. He was walking along the faded center stripe of a two-lane paved road. Gradually, I made out familiar portions of the landscape. First, I saw the water tower that rises to greet people when they drive into town on the west side. Then, the creature moved past the old dairy store, with its fallen-down barn and vine-covered silo. Eventually, he reached my neighborhood.

I tried a variety of cures to banish the nightmares. On the chance that a full stomach was the cause, I skipped dinner.

That wasn't easy. I had to pretend I was sick to get away with that one. I went right up to bed, even though that was the last place I wanted to be. My mother watched me carefully the next day.

"You seem pale," she'd said.

Of course I'm pale. A demon is coming for me.

I didn't share my thoughts.

I tried staying awake. You can't dream when you're awake, of course. But that's not a long-term solution. And the more tired I was when I slept, the more frightening the inevitable dream.

And, always, there were those words: *I'm coming for you.*

Eventually, he reached my front door. I knew my next dream would be unbearable. I stayed awake for two nights. On the third evening, I realized my only hope was to try to slay my demon. I took my drawing pad and my pencils to bed with me. As the sun set, I started to draw.

I sketched a rough outline first, just the way I'd been taught. The eye flows from left to right because that's how we read. I put the monster on the right, full height, blocking the eye from leaving the page. I put myself, in armor, swinging a two-handed broadsword, on the left. The eye follows the sword from the hero to the target. I slay my demon.

I draw, filling in the details. If I can draw it well enough—real enough—I know it will become real and I will slay the demon.

As much as I am focused on my art, I also glance at the clock.

Inevitably, 2 A.M. arrives.

I keep drawing.

Downstairs, the front door swings open. The nightmare progresses, though I am awake.

I've finished the demon. I hurry to complete myself.

The footsteps on the stairs move with excruciating slowness. I'm grateful for the time to finish my work, but I hate the drawn-out terror.

My door bursts open.

I roll from the bed and thrust the drawing in front of myself, using it as a talisman to slay the demon.

He looks up at me.

Up?

His armor glows with the light of righteousness. I drop the pad and stare at my own hands, covered with dull-red flesh. I raise my clawed hands as he swings his broadsword.

The sword strikes.

I am slain.

WIPEOUT OF THE WIRELESS WEENIES

Clickita-clickita-tappity-tap-tap.

It was all around me. Clicks, taps, and flashes of light rose from every seat as images of all sorts flickered across tiny screens. Everyone had a smartphone except me. All the kids in class had them. So did the teacher. She was so busy texting, she didn't even notice all the other texters, surfers, and gamers. The whole world had turned into Wireless Weenies, sucking gigabytes of data out of the air.

I looked down at my work sheet. Even there, I was the only student who wasn't wirelessly wired to the Internet, with its wealth of answers and information. I had to do the work myself. So they all had lots of extra time for their phones after they did their work.

It just wasn't fair.

I'd asked, begged, pleaded, and reasoned with my parents, trying to get a phone. I'd failed. The closest I ever got was, "We'll see, Amanda." More often, the answer was, "Not right now." It all felt like "never." As much as I mocked the Wireless Weenies, I wanted to be one of them.

I was only about halfway through the work sheet when I noticed movement outside the window. Something was pushing up through the ground. The asphalt in the parking lot bulged. Cars started to slide as the hill rose higher. Finally, the ground burst open.

A creature that looked sort of like a cross between a squid and an amoeba flowed through the cratered opening and rippled toward the school.

"Hey!" I shouted.

Everyone looked up from phones and mini tablets.

"A monster!" I pointed out the window.

"Awesome!" Danny Harker said. "I'll put it on YouTube." He raced out the door, followed by three other boys and two girls.

Once they reached the parking lot, they ran toward the creature, their hands thrust out like vampire hunters wielding crosses. They captured some awesome video.

Then the creature captured them. It wasn't pretty, but it was pretty fast. It wrapped tentacles around them and pulled them into its flowing body.

"Got it!" Tom Lanslow said, leaning out the window with his phone aimed at the creature.

The creature kept coming, moving toward the school.

There were some screams now, but there was a lot more clicking, scrolling, and tapping.

"I'll Google 'squid monsters,'" Eric Loomis said, swiping his finger across the screen of his tablet.

"No!" Mike Trujilo said, "go straight to Wikipedia. It's way better."

"I have a monster ID app," Braydon Clark said. He moved closer to the window and pointed the back of his phone at the creature.

Eric and Mike crowded around Braydon, all furiously searching for information.

Then all three were plucked from the window.

"Get out of here!" I shouted toward the rest of the class.

Nobody listened. They were all texting their friends, calling their parents, or searching for a way to survive a monster assault.

I went up front to see what our teacher was doing. I glanced over her shoulder. She was on the teacher's union Web site, looking up what the penalty was for abandoning her students.

I'd seen enough. I headed for the hall. It was crowded with kids. They were all on their phones.

I pushed my way through the crowds. "This way!" I shouted. "Go out the back. We'll be safe if we head that way." It was only a quarter mile to the park, which was bordered on one side by a dense stretch of woods. Unlike us, the creature wouldn't be able to fit among the trees.

Or would it?

I had a moment of doubt. I looked around. There were plenty of kids with smartphones. Maybe one of them could look it up. What would be the best search term? *Can giant squids get through forests? Squid flexibility?*

I shook my head. That was ridiculous. It was better to take my chances than waste time trying to find out.

I heard a crash as the monster broke down the side of the building.

"Come on!" I shouted one last time. "This way!"

None of the Wireless Weenies followed me. I ran out the back door and headed for the woods.

When I got there, I stopped to catch my breath.

The school was a mess. The police showed up a couple minutes later. Then the army came in helicopters.

The choppers had a pretty easy time destroying the monster. I saw a replay of it on the news that night.

My parents were so relieved that I'd survived, they wouldn't stop hugging me. I figured I could get anything I wanted, just by asking for it. I thought about asking for a phone. But that seemed pretty pointless now. There wasn't anybody left for me to call.

SHELL SHOCKED

A midnight swim seemed like an awesome idea until the turtle bit me. It was just our second night at the cabins. There were seven of us. My brother Jake and I were there with our folks. Our neighbors, Mr. and Mrs. Yawinski, were there with their three kids. The Flackners, who we run into every year, were there with Kent, and the Baldridges were there with Mitch. We were staying in the cabins for a whole month. My mom had to work during the week, but she came back for the weekends. So did Mr. Flackner.

It was Kent who suggested we go for a swim. Our folks didn't mind, as long as we promised to keep an eye on each other. The weather was clear. The air was warm. Only Mitch tried to weasel out of it.

"It's not safe," he told Kent. "We won't be able to see anything."

"No clouds tonight," Kent said. "And the moon will be full. There will be plenty of light." He was a big astronomy fan. He knew the constellations and even where to look to spot satellites. So I wasn't surprised he kept track of the moon.

"I'm not going," Mitch said.

So, naturally, when it started to get dark, the six of us grabbed him and carried him to the lake. But he got loose before we could throw him in.

The sun was down by then. Kent was right—it was fun swimming in the dark. But then, about an hour later, when I was just floating on my back, staring up at the stars, something bit my foot, right on the heel.

"Owwww!"

I yelled and tried to stand up. That's not possible in water that's just deep enough to cover your head. I swam for shore, afraid I'd get bitten again.

But I made it out okay.

"What's wrong?" Jake called.

"Something bit me." I climbed up on the bank and twisted my leg so I could see my heel. "It's bleeding," I said.

"Maybe it's time to get out," Jake said.

"It was probably a rock or something," Kent said.

"I guess. . . ." I wasn't sure. I hated to leave, but I didn't like the idea of another bite. Still, it wasn't bleeding all that much. I'd cut myself worse than that sliding into second. I sat on the bank and watched the others swim. I figured I could hang out there until they got tired.

Later, I saw something climb out of the water about fifty yards away. It was too far to tell for sure, but it looked like a large turtle. I didn't feel like getting up and checking. I was feeling sort of tired. So I stayed where I was.

Finally, everyone was ready to head back. I went right to sleep. I didn't even think to look at my heel until the next morning. It wasn't all that bad. I'd definitely been bitten, but the wound had closed up. I washed it when I went into the bathroom, but I figured that by then, it didn't really matter. Any germs had already had plenty of time to do their damage. But it looked like I'd been lucky. There wasn't even any swelling.

We kidded Mitch about cutting out on us. But he's a good guy, and the best ballplayer in the group, so we didn't mock him too hard. The next time Kent suggested swimming at night, two or three days later, Mitch went right along. Nobody got bitten that time. Nobody got bitten the week after that, either.

The vacation was almost over when Kent suggested one final nighttime swim. Once again, Mitch tried to get out of it.

"You're going," I said. "We've been together all summer. You can't wimp out on us now."

"I don't feel good," he said.

"I don't believe you."

He walked off. When we were getting ready to head out to the lake, I looked for him in his cabin, but he wasn't there.

"Go ahead," I told the other guys. "I'm going to find Mitch." I was pretty sure I could do that. I've learned all sorts of woodcraft. A couple years ago, I even took a course in tracking.

So, before the sunlight faded totally, I looked for signs of his passage.

It turned out to be pretty easy to spot his trail. He'd gone downhill, away from the lake. I jogged along until I heard him ahead of me. The moon was just starting to rise when I reached the old road. He'd already crossed it. I saw him disappearing into the brush on the other side.

I stepped onto the road. "Mitch, wait."

He turned back.

I wasn't sure what I expected him to say. I definitely didn't expect him to scream, "Get out of the road!"

That was silly. I doubt a car came along more than two or three times an hour. Besides, the road ran straight for a long way in each direction. If a car were coming, I'd see the headlights and hear it in plenty of time.

"Come on," I said, "let's go swimming."

"Get out of the road!" he screamed again. "Now!"

I took another step toward him. "What are you talking about?"

He pointed past me, toward the horizon. The moon was almost fully visible. "I'm a wereturtle," he said.

That was so silly, I had to laugh. "Yeah, right. And I'm a vampire hippopotamus. Come on." I took another step toward him. Or tried to. My legs felt funny.

"I bit you," he said. "I'm sorry. It's not a big deal. You'll just turn into a turtle during the full moon. Now, would you please get out of the—"

He never finished his sentence. He fell forward. So did I. I could see my hands changing. My arms contracted. Something heavy pressed down on my back. A shell. I tried to move. It was awkward. I'd never walked with flippers, and I'd never been so close to the ground. I pulled myself forward.

I barely moved. I was unused to walking this way. And a turtle, even an experienced one, is already unbearably slow.

I was so busy trying to get off the road, I didn't even notice the truck at first.

Luckily, it passed over me.

The second one didn't.

It crushed my shell and flung me from the road.

I landed in a crumpled heap. I was in human form again. I'd seen enough werewolf movies to know what that meant. I didn't have long. I could feel my strength draining.

I heard a rustling to my left. I looked over. Mitch was there. He was still a turtle. His head and front legs moved in a funny way. I realized it was a shrug. For some reason, that made me laugh. Then everything started to fade.

FEED THE KITTY

I once counted seventeen cats in Mrs. Schuster's front yard. I figured there were probably even more than that. Cats are hard to count when they're skittering all over the place, running across the lawn, climbing the trees, slinking under the rust-spotted car in the driveway, and leaping at each other from ambush positions.

I'd never seen Mrs. Schuster leave the house. She'd come onto the porch to put out bowls of food, but that was as far as she went. I'd never seen her on the sidewalk, or in any of the stores in town. So I was surprised when she walked onto the playground. I was even more surprised when she sat down on a bench near the basketball court and watched our game.

Right after we finished our four-on-four half-court game, she got up and approached us.

"I wonder what she wants?" I said.

"Who cares. She's crazy," Rupert Watson said.

"No, she isn't," I said. "She just likes cats."

Rupert threw the ball at my head. I dodged to the side, but the ball smacked my shoulder. "Ow! What was that for?"

"You called me a liar," Rupert said.

I was about to argue, but Rupert's eyes got that dangerous look. I knew the wrong words would get me punched in the face.

By then, Mrs. Schuster had reached us. "I'm going away for several days," she said. "My sister is having an operation and she'll need my help around the house."

Her voice was surprisingly strong and clear. I'd expected it to be some sort of hoarse croak or faint whisper.

"Who cares?" Rupert said.

Mrs. Schuster went on as if she hadn't heard him. "I need someone to feed my kitty." She held up a fistful of money. "I'll pay one of you young men to do it."

I was about to say, "I love cats," but I only got as far as the first word when Rupert gave me a shove and said, "I'll do it. I'm perfect for the job."

Mrs. Schuster nodded. "Good. I agree—you're perfect. Come to my house when you're finished playing." She told him her address, and then left.

I glared at Rupert—after I was sure his back was turned toward me. This was so unfair. I was good with animals. My aunt had two cats. I took care of them whenever she went out of town. I didn't just dump some food in a bowl and dash out—I played with them and petted them. And I walked my neighbor's dog when he had to work late. He trusted me enough to give me a key to his house. Rupert didn't even have pets. I think his parents were afraid he'd hurt any living creature he got his hands on.

When we were finished playing, I followed Rupert. Maybe he'd mess up, and I could get the job. Or at least I could make sure he didn't hurt any of the cats. He was the sort of kid who would probably kick a small animal if nobody was looking.

When Rupert reached Mrs. Schuster's front porch, I sneaked down the driveway, slipped behind her car, and listened. Rupert knocked on the door. I heard it open.

"When do I get paid?" he asked.

I heard the crinkle of bills. That was a mistake. If he got his money now, there was a good chance he'd never do the job. I wanted to warn Mrs. Schuster, but I didn't want to get Rupert angry with me. If I had to, I'd buy the cats some food, myself.

"Come in, so you can get started," Mrs. Schuster said.

The door shut. I moved closer to the porch. I could still hear them talking.

"Hey—you said you'd pay me to feed your kitty. But there are tons of cats in the yard," Rupert said. "I need more money."

"Don't worry. You have more than you'll possibly be able to spend," Mrs. Schuster said.

"No way," Rupert said. "You have to pay me a lot more than this to feed all your cats."

The door opened again. I saw Mrs. Schuster step onto the porch. "Oh, those aren't my kitties," she said. "These are just visitors. My kitty is too big to be allowed outside. He gets so very hungry. Thank you for feeding him."

She stepped all the way out and shut the door. Then she pulled a large, old-fashioned key out of her pocket, slipped it into the large, old-fashioned keyhole, and locked the door with a solid click.

"Hey!" Rupert shouted. I saw the knob rattle.

There was a loud growl from inside, and then a giant bang

as something slammed into the door. Actually, I think it wasn't just something slamming into the door—I think it was something slamming Rupert into the door.

There were a couple smaller thumps, and a variety of screams. But the cries didn't last long. After that, I could swear I heard purring.

I was frozen to the spot, staring at the locked door, even when Mrs. Schuster walked down the porch steps. She turned toward me. "Kitty has to eat," she said.

"I guess so."

"And that young man seemed like someone who is mean to cats."

"I think you're right," I said. "And not just cats."

"So I'm glad he wanted to feed my kitty," she said. She gave me a wink, then headed toward her car. A dozen cats chased after her.

I guess animals really liked her. So did I.

MUMMY CHASE

I need to catch my breath. I feel like my lungs have been rubbed with sandpaper and filled with acid. But I can't stop. I have to keep running, or I'm doomed.

I never should have swiped the sacred ankh out of the mummy's tomb when I was on vacation with my parents in Egypt. I thought I could get away with it. I managed to sneak it out of the country in my suitcase. I know it's wrong to steal, but I was tired of being a total loser in school every time we did show-and-tell. I never had anything good to bring in. Until now.

When I stole the mummy's ankh, I hadn't counted on supernatural powers and ancient curses. That's a bad combination. The mummy came after me. I guess it was the mummy from that tomb, though it really doesn't matter. Having any mummy chasing you is definitely not a good thing. He showed up about an hour ago, right after dinner. I saw him through the big living room window, stumbling across my front yard. I thought about tossing the ankh to him and hoping that would be enough. But I had a feeling he was looking for a lot more payback. I ran out the back door.

I've been trying to get away ever since, but no matter how fast I run, and how slowly he seems to shuffle after me, I just can't seem to escape.

I have to stop again, just for a second. I can barely breathe. I hate to look back, but I need to see how far away he is. Oh, no. He's less than half a block from me. He'll never give up. I'm flesh and blood. Tired, sweaty flesh and blood, with little breath left. He's bandages and magic. Tireless magic that will never give up. I don't know what he'll do when he catches me, but I know it won't be nice.

I dig deep for more strength and start jogging again. I stopped trying to run fast. Fast or slow, he keeps up with me. So I've been jogging. But even that takes a lot of energy. We're near the edge of town. That's when I see my only hope.

I check my pockets. Yeah. I have enough quarters. I glance back again, even though I don't have to. I know he'll follow me. And I think he might fall for it. He's ancient and wise, but I'd bet he doesn't know anything about modern life or about all of the inventions that came along in the thousands of years since he'd been wrapped up and shoved into a tomb. I guess I'm betting my own life on his ignorance.

I race to the entrance of the car wash and put my change in the coin slot. The water starts spraying. I walk in and move through that part as quickly as I can. I get soaked with hot water, but I don't care. The mummy will get soaked, too. I suspect he won't care, either. All he cares about is catching me and getting revenge.

This better work. It should. Everything depended on a lesson I'd learned the hard way, just last month. I move past the spray to the drying area, where the light from the heat lamps overhead is almost blinding. Hot air blasts at me from both walls and the floor. My T-shirt starts to feel tight across my shoulders. That's the first sign that I might actually survive.

I stop at the far end and look back. The mummy is there—dripping wet at the edge of the spray. He steps into the heat. As he moves toward me, I can see my plan working. Like a soaked sweater tossed into a clothes dryer, the mummy is starting to shrink. That's the lesson I'd learned when Mom made me help with the laundry. She'd been really unhappy about the wool sweater after I'd put it in the dryer. Apparently, you're not supposed to do that with certain types of cloth. I'd gotten in even more trouble when I started laughing at the sight of it. It was ridiculously small.

With each step beneath the heat lamps, the mummy shrinks a bit. Pretty soon he's half his original size, and then even smaller. By the time he reaches me, he's the size of a toddler.

I stand there and stare down at him. He stretches his arms out toward my neck to strangle me, and I can't help laughing. There's no way he can reach that high. He flails at my legs. It doesn't hurt, even when he reaches up and smacks my knee. I'm laughing so hard now, my stomach hurts. He's a whole lot funnier than a shrunken sweater.

I pick him up and tuck him under my arm. He weighs less than a puppy. I don't even care about the ankh anymore. Not now that I have a shrunken mummy. That's pretty awesome. I can't wait for next Tuesday at school. This is going to be the best show-and-tell ever.

BEING GREEN

Bethany decided it was her job to save the planet. Her parents and their friends had obviously messed things up to the point where they couldn't be trusted. But that was all about to change.

"We're recycling," she told her father as she dragged a green plastic bin with the arrow-chasing-itself-in-a-triangle logo into the kitchen. "Clean glass, plastic, and metal go in here." She pointed to a smaller bin on the kitchen counter. "Compostable materials go in here. Vegetable peels, stuff like that. A little bit of paper is okay."

"What about Styrofoam?" her dad asked.

"We aren't using that anymore," Bethany said. "If you must use a disposable container for your coffee, use cardboard."

Her father sighed, but he didn't argue. This was not Bethany's first campaign to make things better.

Bethany's mother also greeted the news with little resistance, though compliance was not perfect. Both parents told her they weren't trading in their perfectly reasonable four-year-old gasoline-powered car for a battery-operated vehicle.

"I'm not driving to work in a glorified golf cart," her dad said. "I have to do battle with trucks every day on the interstate."

It's a start, Bethany thought as she filled her water bottle from the kitchen sink. That was the thing she was proudest of—she wasn't planning to ever drink another bottle of store-bought water. She shuddered at the thought of all that plastic being used and discarded. Her new bottle—a green and white striped ceramic bottle with a rubber stopper and built-in drinking straw, hand-painted by craftsmen in an African village who were raising money to buy a water pump for their well—was the perfect symbol of the new world, the bright green world, she planned to help build. She'd bought it with her own money, along with a second bottle to give to her best friend, Gia.

Bethany sipped her water as she walked to Gia's house. Fresh tap water tasted so much better than that bottled stuff. *Everyone should have a bottle like this.* She couldn't wait to give Gia her present.

The instant the door opened, Bethany held up the paper bag. "I got you something."

"For me?" Gia took the bag and peeked inside. "A water bottle. Cool! It's so pretty. Thanks."

"We're saving the planet," Bethany said.

"Come on in," Gia said. "I'm unplugging all the chargers and power supplies. They suck up so much energy."

"For sure." Bethany followed Gia around the house. As Gia unplugged each power supply, Bethany watched the small red power light wink out like a dying coal.

After dealing with all the power supplies, the girls decided to go for a bike ride. Bethany refilled her water bottle. She didn't rinse it or wash it out. That didn't seem necessary to her. It was just water, after all, so rinsing it would be wasteful.

The next day, after checking with all the stores on Main Street to make sure they were recycling, Bethany and Gia played basketball with their friends at the park. Bethany couldn't help frowning at the girls who brought water in plastic bottles. She'd filled her bottle at home, and then refilled it twice from the water fountain. The bottom of the fountain looked a little green, but Bethany was careful not to let her bottle touch that part.

She forgot to empty the bottle when she got home, but she remembered the next morning when she grabbed it to fill it up before heading out. She didn't waste the water by pouring it down the drain. She drank every drop that was in the bottle, then filled it with fresh water from the tap.

She went to the garage and slung a whole bag of crushed aluminum cans over her shoulder. *I'm making the world green*, she thought as she pedaled her bike to the recycling center.

The facility was at the top of a long road that ran uphill nearly all the way. It was hard pedaling that far in the heat. Bethany was glad she had her water bottle clipped to her bike. She stopped three times to take a drink before she reached the recycling center. But the water wasn't helping a lot. Her mouth felt strange, like her tongue was fuzzy.

When she reached the center, she got off her bike, grabbed the bag of cans, and took it to the huge container for aluminum. There was a set of metal stairs at the side of the container. Bethany climbed up the steps and emptied the bag into the container.

The sun felt brutally hot. As she walked back down the steps, she rubbed her tongue against the top of her mouth.

Everything definitely felt weird. She stuck out her tongue and tried to look at it, but that turned out to be impossible. So she scraped the nail of her index finger across it.

"Green?" she said as she stared at her finger. She had something thick and green under her nail. It almost looked like moss. *Something's wrong with me,* she thought. *I'd better get home.* She tried to run to her bike, but she felt even more sluggish, and could barely walk. When she finally got there, she leaned over, stuck out her tongue, and examined it in the rearview mirror of her bicycle.

Her whole tongue was coated with something thick and green. So was the roof of her mouth and, as far back as she could see, her throat.

I need to rinse my mouth.

She grabbed the water bottle, took a big swig, swished the water in her mouth, then spat it on the ground.

The liquid—there was no way she could call it water—lay in a splatted puddle on the bare earth. It was too thick to sink below the surface immediately, or to evaporate in the rays of the hot sun.

That's what I was drinking?

Bethany dropped the bottle. It shattered, allowing more of the liquid to ooze out. The inside of the bottle was also covered with a thick green coating.

Bethany staggered away from the spot, turned aimlessly for a moment as she tried to figure out what to do, then backed against one of the containers.

"Feel funny," she managed to say before she sank to the ground.

The thick feeling was spreading. She hoped someone would come by and help her.

Time passed. Bethany suspected she might have napped for a while. She tried to look around, but her head didn't seem to move.

Everything looks green.

It was almost as if a thin layer of greenness covered her eyes. She could see her legs stretched out in front of her. The skin of her legs, below her shorts, was green and fuzzy. So was the hem of her shorts.

She dozed again. A voice woke her. It came from less than a yard away, but it sounded distant and muted.

Finally, someone who'll help me.

"You'd think that people who care enough to recycle would care enough to put things in the containers and not just dump them on the ground," the man said. He was wearing a T-shirt with BRENTSFORD COUNTY RECYCLING DEPT. written on the front.

Bethany thought about the broken water bottle. She was sorry she'd left it on the ground. She didn't even know ceramics could be recycled. She thought they weren't considered glass.

The man leaned toward her. "Looks like it's up to me."

I'm saved.

"Here we go." He lifted her. As she rose, she saw a sign on the container she'd rested against. YARD WASTE.

The man dropped her inside.

"Making the Earth a little better place, one small piece at a time" he said, his voice cheerful and satisfied, as he walked away, leaving Bethany with the lawn clippings, pruned branches, and other bits of greenery.

FIRST CONTACT

The alien spaceship landed in my backyard. *Landed* is a bit too gentle a word for the way the football-shaped craft slammed into the ground and dug a twenty-foot-long trench. *Backyard* is a bit too small a word for the farmland that stretches for hundreds of acres behind my house.

Dad was out at the feed store. Mom had gone to the vet's over in Sutter to pick up some medicine for one of our horses. So it was just me and my little brother, Marty, at home when the ship landed. We were out front, in the rocking chairs with a satisfying pile of curled shavings at our feet. I'd been showing Marty how to whittle the bark off a stick with a jackknife without cutting off any fingers. The trick is to always cut *away* from your hand. He was getting the hang of it pretty well when the crash shook the house.

"Whoa—what was that?" I shouted. I folded my knife and rushed straight through the house to the backyard. I got all the way to the back porch before I slid to a halt, my mouth wide open.

"Spaceship," Marty said. He's pretty smart, and he watches a lot of movies.

"Looks like it," I said.

From what I could see, the spaceship was buried about a third of the way down. At least it hadn't wiped out any of the corn. Of course, if it had landed fifty yards south of where it hit, it would have wiped out me and Marty.

"Think there are aliens inside?" Marty asked.

"Maybe. But they could be a bit shook up." I tried to imagine what it would feel like to be on the wrong side of that landing. Unless they had some sort of high-tech shock-absorption system, they had to be a bit rattled. "Let's wait a couple minutes before we start thumping on it."

We waited. I thought about knocking on the outside of the ship, but I'd seen too many movies where the first person the aliens notice gets vaporized with an energy beam. After a while, I heard a scraping sound. Then a hatch flipped open on top. Something peeked over the rim from inside, then climbed out the opening.

"Yeah," I said, "that's an alien."

He—or it—had one thick leg that branched into four parts about midway to the ground. Those parts ended in rippling things at the bottom. The body was round, and just slightly flattened in front. It had two arms, almost no neck, and a head that was sort of cylinder shaped. The hands were empty. Good. No ray guns or mind-control beams. It was wearing some kind of long shirt that was white with large black splotches on it.

I wondered how we were going to communicate. Is there a universal hand signal that means "Your landing skills stink"? Maybe it wouldn't be necessary. If they could get here from another star system, they had to have some amazing technology. I nodded, smiled, then pointed to myself and said, "I am Thad."

The eyes blinked. The alien looked at me and said, "Hello, Thad. I am Jreglitz. What's up, dude?"

"You speak English?"

"We listened to your television and radio broadcasts while we approached." He stepped away from the hatch and slid down the side of the ship, all the way to the ground. A puff of black dust drifted from his body when he came to a stop. Six more aliens just like him followed. Their clothes were covered with some sort of black powder.

"You must be quick learners," I said. "How long was your trip?"

He started to speak, then turned toward one of the others and whispered something. They had a quick discussion. "Seven thousand of your years," he said.

"Seven thousand? That's like forever. How'd you manage that?" I asked. I hate when I have to wait five minutes for one of my shows to start, or two minutes for something to heat up in the microwave. Waiting seven thousand years would be unbearable, even if I had a ton of good books and video games to keep me busy.

"We slept a lot," he said. "It helped pass the time."

I looked at the ship. "So you don't have any kind of hyperspeed engine, or warp drive?"

"No. Our efforts in that direction have all failed. We were hoping you Earthlings would have developed something like that by the time we arrived. Otherwise, our return trip will be equally long. We have seen your space movies, and you seem to have many advanced types of technology."

"What kind of fuel did you use?" I asked. Maybe they at least had some sort of nuclear thing going. Better yet, they could have some totally new form of energy that we hadn't discovered, yet. This could change the world.

"Coal," he said.

"Coal?" I asked.

"Coal." He patted his chest, sending up another black cloud of dust. "We needed a lot of it. It's heavy, but it's cheap. We used to use wood, but coal is so much more advanced."

I looked over at Marty. "Anything you want to ask them about?"

"You think they have some kind of cool weapon we could try? . . ."

"They use coal to crawl between the stars at an agonizingly slow pace," I said. "They probably fight with sticks and rocks. I suspect they'd be terrified if I showed them my laser pointer."

"Then I can't think of anything to ask them," he said.

"Me neither." I checked my watch. Our favorite show, *Space Cadets Conquer the Universe,* was on in two minutes. I definitely didn't want to miss that.

"Can you take us to your leader?" Jreglitz asked.

I headed for the door. "Sure. Later. We'll be back in a little while. You don't mind waiting, do you?" There really didn't seem to be any rush.

"We're very good at that," Jreglitz said, taking a seat on the ground.

"Excellent." I went inside with Marty and turned on the TV, eager for some real alien excitement.

BARK LIKE A DUCK

Julie suspected something was up the instant Mrs. Lahasca bounced into the classroom. "Boys and girls," the teacher said, ringing her favorite little bell to get their attention, "I have some absolutely unbelievable news."

Eighteen pairs of eyes turned toward their teacher. Eighteen pairs of lips began whispering and exchanging guesses. "Maybe we're going on a trip," Julie said to Kris, who sat at the desk to her right. "That would be fun."

"Hope so," Kris whispered back.

"Class!" Mrs. Lahasca tinkled the bell a bit harder and waited. Finally, when the whispering settled down from full sentences to single words, she continued. "We have been chosen, just us out of all the schools in Pennsylvania, to become a test site for the new Rubinsky Immersion Method."

The joy and anticipation drained from Julie. She could hear the capital letters in her teacher's voice. She waited for the rest of the news.

Mrs. Lahasca seemed to be struggling to spew the words out rapidly enough to convey the magnitude of her enthusiasm.

"It started in California, and now they're ready to share it with the rest of the world. Think of it, the Rubinsky Immersion Method. History will never be the same. No more boring memorization. No more facts that have no meaning. We are going to live the history."

"Cool," Julie said. Her own enthusiasm sprang back to life. She imagined what it would be like, and wondered if they would be getting costumes. As her fantasies played out in her mind, she thought she heard her teacher saying something about animals.

"What was that?" she whispered to Kris.

Kris just shook her head and said, "No, she's kidding."

Julie turned her attention back to the teacher. As she listened, she realized that Mrs. Lahasca was indeed talking about animals.

"Now, this is very complicated, and will only make real sense to someone who has studied education," the teacher said, grinning a bit. "Rubinsky, who holds degrees in education, history, psychology, and agriculture, has determined that the true experience of history is best viewed by the animals who are observing the people, since they are impartial. That means they haven't already formed an opinion. They are unbiased. And we, using the Rubinsky Immersion Method, will emulate the animals."

"Emulate?" Julie asked out loud.

Mrs. Lahasca, in her enthusiasm, allowed the interruption. "Yes, we will play the roles of the relevant animals. As we study the Pilgrims, we will see them through the eyes of sheep and geese. We will view the Revolutionary War through the eyes of the horses. Imagine—for the first time since the dawn of education, we will learn history as it was meant to be learned."

Billy Mitchell raised his hand and squirmed the way boys do when they want to be called on.

"Yes, Billy, what is it?"

"Can I be a dog?"

The teacher smiled, as if this were a reasonable request. "You will get to be all kinds of animals. We'll all get a chance to be many things." She lifted a box onto her desk. "Now, for a start, we will all be sheep." She pointed to Julie. "Would you please pass out a sheep kit to each student."

Julie nodded. *Sheep kit?* she wondered. She moved along the aisles, handing each student a large envelope labeled POST PLYMOUTH SHEEP SIMULATION DEVICES—RUBINSKY NUMBER HA7-35.A. When she was done, Julie sat and opened her own pack. It contained a piece of wool on a strap, earmuffs, and special eyeglasses.

She followed the instructions that her teacher read from the manual. The muffs and glasses were supposed to let her hear and see the world the way a sheep would. The wool was for her to touch and hold whenever she wasn't feeling sheepish.

While Julie and her classmates crawled on the floor and made *baaaaaa* sounds, Mrs. Lahasca walked among them, carrying cardboard cutouts of famous Pilgrims, and made conversations, doing all the voices herself. Julie suspected her teacher wasn't really very good with voices, but the way the earmuffs muffled everything, it was hard to tell.

By the end of the day, Julie had sore knees and a dislike of wool. By the end of the week, she was certain she'd gag if anyone in her presence used anything containing lanolin.

The next week, she got to be a cow. The week after that, she was a pig. Somewhere along the line, Julie decided to become a vegetarian.

Finally, after the class had received a month of intense instruction, Mrs. Lahasca announced that it was time for a test. "Rubinsky believes that information should be thoroughly absorbed before any testing. But the time has come."

The class groaned as the teacher handed out the tests. Julie looked at the first question: "Name three influential Pilgrim leaders."

She picked up her pen. *That's easy,* she thought. *Baa,* she wrote. Then *Baaaa,* and *Baaaaa.*

Julie zipped through the test. She realized that, while the method might have been a bit uncomfortable, it had taught her a lot. And she was really looking forward to the next session. They were all going to learn about the *Monitor* and the *Merrimack,* the two ironclad Civil War battle ships, from the viewpoint of fish.

THE RAREST OF MONSTERS

Most kids are afraid of the guy who runs the used book store, because he always looks angry. I don't like him, but he doesn't scare me. So I go there when I'm looking for something to read. I was searching through the paperback horror novels Saturday afternoon, down on my knees, going through the bottom shelf where they stash the cheapest ones. That's how I ended up following Grungy home. That's what we call him. Grungy. I don't know his real name. I don't care. I didn't even know he could talk until he came into the shop.

"Anything?" he asked the owner.

"Just got a couple boxes from an estate sale," the owner said, pointing toward the back of the shop. "Haven't even sorted them yet."

Grungy scurried down the aisle to the back. As always, winter or summer, he was wearing a stained, ripped coat and heavy work boots. It was the middle of August, so the coat definitely wasn't a good idea. I was wearing a T-shirt, and I was sweating. But Grungy didn't seem to notice the heat. I ignored him as I continued to dig among the shelves. About five minutes later, I heard a gasp, like he'd been kicked in the stomach. Then I heard Grungy mutter, "I never thought I'd find it."

He stopped talking after that, but I could hear him breathing real fast, like he was super excited about something and trying to calm down.

After a while, he took the book up front. "How much?" I noticed he didn't put it down on the counter. I could tell he didn't want to let go of it for even a second.

"*Rare Monsters*," the owner said, as if weighing the value of the words. He named a price—a very high price. It was my turn to gasp, but Grungy didn't even flinch.

He pulled a wallet from his pocket and paid for the book, handing over as much as I'd made all last summer. Then he left the shop. I followed. I didn't have any plan. I wasn't going to snatch the book from him—though I have to admit that idea did come to mind before I pushed it away. But I wasn't ready to accept that the mystery would remain unsolved. I had to find out what would make a book cost that much.

It turned out Grungy lived in a part of town we called the Wrecks. The houses were falling apart, if they were even standing. I was half a block away from him when I watched him go inside. I waited a moment, then went around the block, cut through some yards, and crept toward his house from the back. It's a good thing the grass and weeds were way too tall and I was stooping real low. Otherwise, I would have been caught. Before I got close to the house, he came out the back door, carrying a small table.

I flattened down and watched. He made three more trips, bringing a chair, a box full of stuff, and then the book. He took a seat and opened the book to the first page.

For half an hour, he just read. Then I heard him say, "This one. Wealth and power."

He headed back into the house. I realized this was my chance, if I wanted to snatch the book, but I figured it was better to wait and see what he was doing.

He pulled a blanket from the box and spread it on the ground, sprinkled a circle of salt around it from a big blue carton like my mom has in the kitchen cabinet, then started reading words out loud from the book in a way that reminded me of singing. The words didn't sound like any language I'd ever heard.

I felt the ground tremble.

Something rose from the center of the cloth. It was like a boy made of swirling sludge. He was half the height of Grungy, but broader. His hands ended in claws.

"Gold," Grungy said. He pointed to a spot next to the cloth.

The creature growled like a cornered dog. Something glittered. I saw a small pile of gold coins on the ground.

"More," Grungy said.

"Once a day," the creature said.

"No matter," Grungy said. "There are many others I can call. I hope you enjoy company." He went back to reading.

I didn't watch him. I watched the creature. It moved to the very edge of the cloth, where the line of salt lay, and glared at Grungy. I had a feeling it wanted to rip him into pieces. I could never have sat there that calmly, reading a book, while that creature watched me.

Eventually, I heard another gasp of satisfaction from Grungy. "Diamonds! With no limit. Perfect." He got up, went inside, and came back with an empty glass and a pitcher of water. He set the glass on the table, filled it, then set down the pitcher.

I watched as he cast another spell. When he was finished, he reached for the glass of water. But the cuff of his sleeve knocked over the pitcher.

The water splashed across the ground, washing away part of the circle of salt. The circle was broken.

The next part was a blur.

Grungy barely managed to let out a scream before the creature leaped from the cloth and attacked him.

I closed my eyes and pressed my palms hard against my ear. When I opened my eyes, Grungy was dead, sprawled across the ground. I held my breath, afraid the creature would spot me.

But he had other plans. "Fool," he said as he scooped up the coins. Then he vanished in a dark puff of smoke.

"Wow . . ."

I was trembling, but I was also excited. Diamonds. That sounded good. I didn't know how I'd sell them, but I could worry about that later. Or look for a safe spell.

I walked over to the table. I realized I was sweating. My face felt hot. I grabbed the glass and took a drink.

"Okay, let's see what kind of monster you are," I said.

I looked at the book, hoping it wasn't in some strange language. But, except for the spell itself, the book was in English. The letters were fancy, and the spelling was strange. But I could make it out.

At the top of the page, in large letters, was written: SALAMANDER AQUAFARIOUS.

Below that, it read: *Will fetch diamonds without limit.*

I read on: *Salamander Aquafarious is translucent when sum-*

moned. It dwells exclusively in fresh water. It is most commonly used by those seeking wealth, though it is also popular among assassins.

My stomach rippled at the word *assassins.*

But I was seeking wealth, not murder. And I would be more careful than Grungy.

I read some more: *Once summoned into a proper receptacle, the salamander will remain in the glass until released. Care must be taken that the innocent or unwary do not drink from the glass. As assassins have learned, this salamander does fatal damage once inside the body.*

I looked at the glass. It was empty. I hadn't realized I'd drunk the whole thing. I pushed the book away and sprang up from the chair. An instant later, a slashing pain in my gut doubled me over.

I fell to my knees as the searing pain traveled from my stomach up to my throat, and then out my mouth.

Something fell to the ground in front of me. My eyes couldn't focus. The pain swelled and wrapped around me. The salamander wriggled toward the puddled water on the ground. It stopped short. I reached out and pushed it forward, into the water.

It disappeared in smoke, leaving me behind to die alone.

CHOOSE YOUR OWN MISADVENTURE

You stand at the front steps of an abandoned house. The paint has flaked off, leaving the outer walls the color of dead rodents. Several boards are missing from the porch, and the door itself is covered with a spiderweb dotted with the fragile husks of lifeless flies and moths. Will you enter the house or will you walk away? If you wish to enter the house, skip to the next paragraph. If you wish to leave, keep reading. You leave the house and go home. You lead an unexciting life and eventually, thanks to your reluctance to take risks, die of boredom. The end.

The door is warped, but you manage to force it open with your shoulder. You step into an old-fashioned parlor with a couch, several chairs, and a small table. Dust fills your nose and lungs, stealing your breath. The floor sags beneath your weight, threatening to break and send you plummeting into the basement. You hear music drifting in from the next room. If you decide to come to your senses and leave, skip over the next paragraph. If you decide to investigate the music, read on.

You find a player piano in the next room. It is playing the

first four notes of "Row, Row, Row Your Boat" over and over. There is a pause at the end of the fourth note. If you feel an irresistible urge to play the fifth and final note of the phrase, skip over the next paragraph. If you come to your senses and leave, keep reading.

You leave, but in your haste to flee, you forget about the missing boards on the porch. You break your leg, losing your starting spot on the team and giving up your starring role in the school play, which goes to your former best friend. You grow sullen and bitter, and eventually become one of those adults who shouts at kids to stay off their lawns. The end.

As you play the missing fifth note, the piano slides away from the wall, revealing hidden stairs that rise out of sight. Do you climb the stairs or do you leave? If you wish to leave, go to the previous paragraph. Otherwise, read on.

You climb the stairs and find yourself in a room with no furniture except a small table, a single chair, and a lamp. There is a book on the table. Do you start to read it or do you leave the room? If you start to read the book, skip over the next paragraph. Otherwise, keep reading.

Your lack of curiosity about the book also keeps you from wondering about the noises you hear behind you as you turn away from the table and descend the stairs. This allows the rats that were lurking there to swarm over you before you can reach the door. You do not live happily ever after, but you made it a good day for the rats.

You pick up the book and start to read a story called "Choose Your Own Misadventure." If you have no interest in reading the whole story, go to the previous paragraph. Otherwise, go back to the first paragraph.

KILLER ID

"I'm going to the store. We're out of milk," Carlie's mom said. "I'll be right back. Don't answer the door for strangers."

"I know," Carlie said. "I'm not a little kid." She could recite all the safety rules from memory. She'd heard them far more often than necessary. It was okay to open the door for someone she recognized. But not for a stranger, no matter how unthreatening the person looked. The same rule held for the phone. She could answer the call if a friend or neighbor was on the other end. But if she saw an unfamiliar name on the caller ID, or if it said UNKNOWN CALLER, she wasn't supposed to pick up the phone.

At least they had caller ID now. Last month, her parents had bought a set of three cordless phones. Finally. The whole time she was growing up, Carlie had to deal with these stupid ancient phones her parents had owned since way back when they first got married. The old phones didn't have a display or anything. No speed dial. No menu. Nothing useful at all.

Worse, they had these twisted cords that were always getting knotted up and tangled. There was one old phone left, on the wall in the kitchen, but the rest were gone.

After begging and pleading for new phones for years, Carlie had finally found a way to get what she wanted. This one kid in her biology class, Luca Raskolni, was good with electronics. He wasn't her friend or anything, but Carlie had discovered that the nerdy, awkward boys in her class were always eager to do what she asked if she smiled at them.

Luca had certainly come through. He'd messed up three of the old phones so it seemed like they were going bad. They'd still worked when he was finished, but a crackle of static made it difficult to understand what people were saying. Luca hadn't had a chance to ruin the phone in the kitchen. He'd had to scoot out the back door when Carlie heard her parents' car in the driveway. But at least, with three phones going bad, Carlie's parents had finally bought replacements that didn't belong in an antique shop.

As soon as her mom left for the store, Carlie went back to watching television. A moment later, the phone rang. There was a handset right next to her on the table by the couch, sitting in a charging cradle. Carlie looked at the caller ID display, hoping one of her friends was on the other end.

UNKNOWN KILLER.

"What?" It took her a second to realize it hadn't said UNKNOWN CALLER.

As the second ring scraped against her nerves, Carlie read the words again. No mistake. And no way she was going to pick up the phone. She inched away from the handset, but kept her eyes on the display and wondered why the room suddenly felt ten degrees colder.

After the fourth ring, the answering machine picked up. Carlie held her breath as she listened to the outgoing message.

"Hi. You've reached the Embersons," her dad's voice said. "We can't take your call right now. Please leave a message after the beep."

There was a click, followed by the hollow silence of a dead connection. No message. Carlie shuddered, but she figured it was some kind of glitch in the phone lines.

Five minutes later, the phone rang again. Carlie was afraid to look at the display, but even more afraid not to look.

KILL WAITING.

"That does it!" Carlie grabbed the phone, slid open the back compartment, and ripped out the battery. The loss of power silenced the phone. But the other phones in the house rang three more times, until the answering machine picked up. Again, there was no message.

All was quiet for the next five minutes. Then the phones rang. Carlie ran to her parents' bedroom and pulled the battery from that phone. The display, before fading, read KILLER APP.

The last cordless phone was in the basement. As Carlie passed through the kitchen, she glanced at the phone on the wall. Suddenly, old-fashioned electronics didn't seem all that stupid or annoying. There was something solid and reliable about the wall phone.

She opened the door to the basement and raced down. The instant her foot hit the bottom step, the phone rang. She grabbed the phone before the second ring. As she struggled to remove the battery cover—a task that turned out to be nearly impossible with trembling hands—she read the message: PHONE KILLER.

"No!" Carlie hurled the phone against the wall and ran back to the kitchen. She stopped at the top of the steps to catch her breath.

The wall phone rang.

Carlie yanked it from the hook and shouted into the mouthpiece, "Stop it! Stop calling!"

There was no answer, but Carlie could tell the line was open. Someone was on the other end.

Just as she was about to hang up, she heard a whisper in the handset. "Carlie? . . ."

"What?" Even that came out as a scream. Carlie tried to stop her hand from shaking, but the tremors resisted her efforts and grew stronger.

"I'm right behind you," the voice whispered.

Carlie spun around and stepped back. The long, twisted phone cord wrapped around her. She grabbed at it with her free hand as she took another step backwards. It tangled around her like a plastic eel.

"Here I come!" This time, the words were shouted.

Carlie staggered farther back. There was nobody in front of her. Unfortunately, there was also nothing beneath her feet. She'd backed through the door to the basement.

Carlie lost her balance. She tumbled and spun down the stairs, until she was jerked to a halt by the cord around her neck. The phone fell from her fingers.

The three cordless phones, despite being dead themselves, all briefly flashed one last message: TOLD YOU SO.

As for the kitchen phone—the line went dead.

A WORD OR TWO ABOUT THESE STORIES

If you've read the other Weenies collections, you know I like to take a little space in the back of the book to talk about where I got the ideas for the stories. (And if you haven't read the other collections, I hope you will feel inspired to do so.)

After the Apocalypse

You know those great birthday parties kids have? They can cause a lot of stress for parents. One year, when our daughter was young, my wife and I offered her a choice of a party or a trip to Disney World. So the idea of parents trying to avoid a party comes from real life. Add to that the huge popularity, right now, of zombies and zombie apocalypses, and the story fell together nicely.

Dead Meat

I like writing the occasional story where a kid gets trapped someplace unpleasant. (See "The Short Cut" in *Invasion of the Road Weenies* for a really scary example of this.) When I started out, all I knew was that I wanted to lock a kid in a butcher shop. Various things could have happened at that point. For example, the kid could have encountered the ghosts of animals. Or he could have had an unpleasant encounter with some of the butcher's tools. But when I was thinking about the meat case, it hit me that all those slabs of muscle and bone were a perfect monster kit.

My New Hat

I was probably in seventh grade when I made the nearly fatal mistake, during a trip with my mom to the B. Altman department store in Short Hills, New Jersey, of selecting a hugely dorky hat. My next appearance at the school bus stop was not pleasant. No aliens appeared in a deus ex machina manner (look it up) to save my hide. The good thing about the traumas of youth is that they can inspire stories. Even better, I can let aliens disintegrate bullies.

Fabrications

I am a science nerd at heart, so it isn't surprising that I came up with "What if a girl created a fabric-eating bacteria to get revenge on a bully?" That might seem like a pretty complex idea to have sprung fully formed from my head. But I can trace its roots back to an earlier idea. When I was in high school, one of my classmates had his blue jeans start to disintegrate. (Not the whole thing—just an area on one leg.) He realized he'd gotten battery acid on them when he was working on his car. So the idea of disintegrating clothing was in the back of my mind, waiting to emerge at the right time.

Plague Your Eyes

Because it is so easy to cut and paste text from the Internet, accidental or intentional plagiarism is a problem in schools. I was reading a discussion of this on a Listserv for librarians when I realized that if a kid stole an author's words, it would be nice payback if the author showed up and stole the kid's words.

Control Issues

I did pick up a wireless controller for my PS2, many years ago. (I actually own a wireless Atari joystick, too.) It does have two parts, one of which plugs into the controller port. I'd toyed with ideas in the past about a kid who finds a controller that actually controls people. Good ideas often come when you combine things. In this case, the wireless idea fit nicely with the control-someone idea.

Mr. Chompywomp

I've seen so many little kids clutching a favorite stuffed animal, it wasn't surprising I'd start to think about what would happen if there was more to the animal than met the eye. After all, just because something is stuffed doesn't mean it's filled with nothing more than stuffing.

Flesh Drive

I started out thinking about a kid who discovers a USB port in his body. (I guess I had flash drives on my mind. I carry my school presentation on one, so I'm always very careful about how I remove it.) At first, I was going to explore various ways he could fill himself with information. But, as I wrote the opening, this less-pleasant ending came to mind. I know I took a chance by ending it in the middle of a sentence, but I trust my readers to understand what I'm doing. And I loved the idea allowing them to enjoy an extra spark of pleasure as they made the connection and realized it wasn't a printing error.

Gothic Horrors

This story began with the idea of black-painted nails turning into insects. I like it when I start out with the idea for the ending. It's a lot easier to think in terms of "How did this come about?" and build toward the existing ending than to take an opening and ask, "What happens next?" while working toward the ending. But both approaches can produce good stories.

In a Class by Himself

Sometimes, a what-if idea is intriguing (what if a kid was the only one in his class), but feels like it might be hard to turn into a story. All the character had to do was ask why he was the only kid in the class. But I liked the potential for absurdity. (I feel that true absurdity is best enjoyed in small doses, which makes it perfect for short stories.) And I liked the idea of the student and teacher both trying to act as if they were in a regular classroom. (You'll notice that what-if plays a large part in my creative process. I actually write a what-if question at the start of each writing day. The file has grown quite large.)

The Dumpster Doll

Not only do I like trapping kids in scary places, I also like trapping them with scary objects. And dolls, along with clowns, are at the top of the list of things that are a lot scarier than they should be. (Hey, I think I need to write a story about a clown doll.)

M.U.B.

One thing I love about writing Weenies collections is that I can write all sorts of different stories, using whatever style or technique I want to explore. In *The Battle of the Red Hot*

Pepper Weenies, the story "Yakity-Yak" is written as a monologue. All we see are the words of the main character. I wanted to write a story using nothing but dialogue. A conversation with the Monster Under the Bed (I trust you may have already figured out what M.U.B. stood for) seemed a perfect platform for this technique.

Sympathy Pains

I had the idea of a kid making a voodoo doll and unknowingly connecting it not to her victim but to herself. I have to confess that it wasn't until I was revising the story (a process I find even more rewarding and creative than writing the first draft) that I realized the irony of having the girl misread the instructions when her intended victim was the reading teacher. Not everything you find in stories and novels is intentional.

Rough Road

When I talk with students about what-ifs, I tell them that some of the best stories happen when you turn the idea around, and make something that seems great (what if I won a million dollars?) turn out to be terrible, or something that seems to be terrible (what if I got hit by a car?) turn out to be wonderful. Having heard so many kids come up with "what if there was no school?" I eventually twisted it into "what if there was a land where kids had to battle their way to school every day?"

No Thanks

I like the idea of aggregating misdeeds. (I like big words sometimes, too.) My first thought for this story was merely that after a kid had failed to send a note a certain number of times, his relatives would take back all the gifts they'd given him. This took a darker twist as I contemplated the full ramifications (oops—sorry, there I go again) of this.

Coffin Fits

This is hard for me to admit, because it shows how dark my thoughts can be, but the story sprang from my idea of a kid actually chewing his way out of a very horrifying situation. I realized there are some stories that are better left unwritten. But one idea led to another, and I decided I could write a story where the character only thinks he's in that situation. It also seemed like a good idea to keep the chewing to a minimum.

Walnuts

Nut allergies are a serious problem. There's nothing funny about having an allergy. So I wasn't sure whether it would be okay to write a story about that issue. But the twist was so delicious, I couldn't resist. Still, I was a bit worried. My first thought was that I could balance things out by having the teacher in the story talk about what a serious problem it is. But we have a word for stories like that. They are *didactic.* A didactic story can come off sounding preachy. In the end, I decided to take a chance. If you are allergic to nuts, I hope you still enjoyed the story. If you aren't allergic to nuts, I hope you realize that those who are allergic have to deal with a serious problem. Be nice to them, or I'm sending the walnuts your way for a visit.

A Litter Bit of Trouble

It's hard to look at a litter box and not think up some sort of monstrous or unpleasant idea. I also tend to be the sort who puts off chores, so I guess I am my own inspiration for this story. At least I didn't put off the task of writing it. And, once the idea of a litter monster hit me, there was no way I could resist bringing it to life.

Moving Stairs

I get lost far too easily, both outdoors and in buildings. (Once, even though I had written directions, a map, and a GPS, I had a hard time finding a school.) So that's where part of the idea comes from. I also have had the unpleasant experience of trying to find someone in a large store with three or four floors. For this story, I just made the store a lot taller.

Matters of Fax

Fax machines and I don't get along all that well, but I have one, because I sometimes need to send or receive something that way. I think I was watching it swallow a piece of paper when the idea for this story hit me.

Casting Magic

I used to fish a lot. If you look at ads in fishing magazines, you'll see phrases like "catch a fish on every cast." That inspired me to think, *What if a kid caught a fish on every cast?* As with most what-ifs, the story could have gone in all sorts of directions, from funny to tragic. But given the competitive nature of far too many fishermen, the path I took seemed like a nice fit. (For a much darker fishing story, check out "A Little Night Fishing" in *In the Land of the Lawn Weenies.*)

Swim Safety

I started out thinking about jellyfish being attracted by peanut butter. From there, it was easy to make the connection with the old rule about not swimming after eating.

Drawn That Way

I'll admit, this is one of my weirder stories. It began with the idea of a monster approaching someone in a series of nightmares. I don't know what gave me the idea for the drawing part. I'll also admit the ending is a bit metaphysical. I can't really explain why the narrator became the demon. But I like that it happened. I figure it's okay, in a collection this large, to toss in something a bit puzzling. But I promise not to do it too often.

Wipeout of the Wireless Weenies

Look around. Wherever there are people, there is talking, texting, swiping, and surfing. Way back when video cameras first became popular, I noticed that some people were so wrapped up in recording their vacations that they never actually *experienced* anything. I still have an old-fashioned flip phone, not because I don't want to have total and constant access to the Internet, but because I know that once I have it, I will be unable to resist the allure of using all that power constantly.

Shell Shocked

Wereturtles. Doesn't everyone think about them all the time? I know I do. Seriously, I have contemplated a huge variety of werecreatures. When turtles crossed my mind, I knew it would be a good variation for a story.

Feed the Kitty

As a cat lover (except when they are coughing up hair balls in the middle of the night), I tend to come up with a lot of ideas about felines. When I realized that "feed the cat" wasn't limited to house pets, I knew I had a story.

Mummy Chase

I get along with washing machines and clothes dryers about as well as I get along with fax machines, so I've inevitably seen my share of shrunken clothing. I also realized I've had only one mummy story in these collections. ("A Tiny Little Piece" in *Invasion of the Road Weenies.*) I figured it was time for another. As I was thinking about mummies, it hit me that they were made of natural fabric. (Okay—they have other stuff on the inside, but this is a fantasy story, so we can pretend none of that exists.)

Being Green

Several years ago, my wife gave me a water bottle that I could take with me to school visits. I liked the idea of a reusable bottle. Unfortunately, I left it at the very next school I visited. (This also explains why, no matter how cold it is, I generally leave my jacket in the car when I reach a school.) So my reusable bottle lasted for one use. But I know a lot of people who manage to hold on to such things for longer. I guess that's what inspired me to write a what-if about a girl who uses a water bottle because she wants to be green, and gets her wish.

First Contact

Another what-if from my files. What if aliens arrived, and they were incredibly boring? This shows a nice thing about what-ifs. Not only can any idea spawn endless stories, but most ideas can be endlessly varied. Fill in the blank: *What if aliens arrived and they were* _________? Made of water, afraid of the color blue, enormous, allergic to concrete, searching for Superman. . . . There really are endless ideas available.

Bark like a Duck

People are always coming up with new ways to teach things. Some of these methods are great; others are terrible. The problem is, the only way to find out is to test them. Unfortunately, this has exposed students to some ridiculous things over the years. When my daughter was in school, I saw my share of bad ideas being forced on students and teachers. That's what inspired this story. As silly as this story might seem, it's not all that far from reality.

The Rarest of Monsters

This began with the idea of a monster that resembled water. Some ideas are hard to execute. (Interestingly enough, *execute* means both "to bring about" and "to eliminate.") I had to figure out how to summon such a monster, and how to put the glass in the hands of the main character, and how to make him drink the water. The same idea could have gone in an entirely different direction if I'd decided to put the monster in a lake or river. Who knows? I may still do that someday.

Choose Your Own Misadventure

Last year, I put together a huge index of topics for all of the Weenies stories from the first five books. (It's at www.davidlubar.com/weenies_index.html. Your teacher will find it much more interesting than you will. I haven't put in the sixth book yet, or this one. As I mentioned, I tend to put off my chores.) As I was working on various language arts topics, I realized I'd never written a Weenies story using second-person viewpoint. This viewpoint is rarely used in fiction, except for choose-your-own-adventure stories. So, naturally, I decided I had to write a misadventurous version of that type of tale.

Killer ID

My mind hands me puns all the time. One day, as I was looking at my caller ID, it told me: UNKNOWN CALLER. And I thought of the phrase *unknown killer.* That was the spark that led to this story.

And that brings us to the end of a lucky seventh collection of warped and creepy tales. I plan to keep writing them. I hope you plan to keep reading. And while you're waiting for that collection, please check out my other books.

READER'S GUIDE

ABOUT THIS GUIDE

The information, activities, and discussion questions that follow are intended to enhance your reading of *Wipeout of the Wireless Weenies*. Please feel free to adapt these materials to suit your needs and interests.

WRITING AND RESEARCH ACTIVITIES

I. Opposites Interact

A. In several stories, the author takes familiar scenarios such as a kid with a "nut allergy" ("Walnuts") or feeding a neighbor's "pet" ("Feed the Kitty") and gives them surprising outcomes. Write a one-paragraph summary for each of these two stories, explaining what you expected from these scenarios after reading the opening paragraphs, and describing the "opposite" results you discovered at the end of the stories.

B. Make a list of other stories from *Wireless Weenies*, as well as titles of other books and story collections you have read, that incorporate a reversal of your expectations through plot, character, or story structure. Write a paragraph explaining why "reversing expectations" might be a good trick to keep in your story-writing toolbox.

C. On a sheet of lined paper, categorize the stories in this collection in terms of pairings or groups of tales that offer opposing perspectives on similar themes or plots. For example, "Sympathy Pains" and "Casting Magic" present two characters with different attitudes toward magical power.

D. With friends or classmates, brainstorm a list of literal and thematic opposites, such as dark/light, friendly/mean, and dog/cat. Vote to select one opposite pairing that sparks many group members' imaginations. Individually, write one-paragraph descriptions of Lubar-style stories inspired by the pairing you selected. Share your results with the group, and discuss the different ways the opposites were interpreted.

II. The Great Unknown

A. In "Matters of Fax," "Smart Phones," "Control Issues," and other stories in this collection, technology plays surprising roles. Write a short essay describing the technology-related story that you found most surprising, interesting, or frightening and why. Or write an essay describing why technological devices make interesting "villains" for today's readers.

B. The *Wireless Weenies* collection is filled with surprising characters, such as a were-turtle. Pick your favorite strange character or story narrator (if s/he survives their story) and write a one-page magazine-style interview in which you ask the character at least three questions you would like them to answer about themselves, their origins, and the way they see the world.

C. In "My New Hat" and "First Contact," extraterrestrial beings encounter human narrators. Imagine you are an "Alien Investigator." Using details from these stories and other alien tales of your choosing, create a PowerPoint presentation entitled "Why Earthlings Shouldn't (or Should) Worry About Extraterrestrials." Present your report to friends or classmates.

III. Collecting Ideas

A. As in his other Weenies collections, David Lubar provides an afterward in which he shares insights about each story's inspiration. Select your favorite story, then flip to the back of the book to read about how the author got the idea to write it. Write a one- to two-paragraph reaction to this information and, if applicable, the way it impacts your reading of the story.

B. "What-ifs" are the starting point for several stories. Keep a "what-if" journal for a week, a month, or longer if desired. Each day, write at least one short "what-if" sentence or phrase. At the end of your journal-keeping time, flip back through your entries and select one to use as the basis for a two- to five-page story.

C. With friends or classmates, brainstorm a list of ways to find story ideas or present a collection of yours (such as baseball cards, rocks, or mystery novels) to friends or classmates and discuss how it might be a starting point for a story.

D. Inspired by Lubar's afterword notes, take the story you have written in exercise III.B., above, and revise it using one of his techniques, such as rewriting it in dialogue or from a second-person viewpoint; increasing the level of absurdity; trapping a character or characters somewhere in the story; or using a deus-ex-machina plot devise to resolve a problem.

E. Imagine you have been hired to design a new, collectible edition of the *Wireless Weenies* book. Review the collection, noting images, themes, colors, or other elements that might help you develop a style for your design. Using colored pencils, paints, or other craft materials, create small illustrations to accompany your five favorite chapter titles. If desired, design a new cover as well.

QUESTIONS FOR DISCUSSION

1. *Wipeout of the Wireless Weenies* is David Lubar's seventh Weenie story collection. Have you read other Lubar anthologies, or other story collections? Have you read other scary books? Did you begin reading this book with certain expectations? Explain your answers.
2. The first story in this collection is dramatically entitled "After the Apocalypse." What are the first few ideas that come into your mind after reading such a title? How did the story turn these ideas around? In what ways does this story show readers what to expect from *Wireless Weenies* tales?
3. In "Fabrications," the narrator finds clever ways to attack braggarts and other "bad kids." Do you think her actions make the narrator a "good kid" or do they make you view her as equally bad? Explain your answer. What other stories in the collection make you reconsider the notion of the "good guy"?

4. "Gothic Horror" begins with Selena's desire to be part of a group of "goth girls." How does this desire play out? Do you have sympathy for Selena? Why or why not? What advice might you give to kids struggling to become part of a school social group?
5. What surprising conclusion does the narrator draw at the end of "Casting Magic?" Do you agree with his choice? If you had access to magic, would you use it? Why or why not?
6. List at least three stories in this collection where bad intentions or actions lead characters to "get what they deserve." List at least three stories where characters try to help someone else or solve a problem. What is similar about the outcomes of these stories? What is different? What rule or rules of behavior might you recommend to all of these characters and why?
7. "Being Green" takes an interesting look at environmental awareness (or lack of awareness). How would you summarize the story in one sentence? How might you revise or rewrite a "green" slogan you have read to ensure that others don't repeat the narrator's mistake?
8. David Lubar admits that he "gets lost far too easily" and that this was part of his inspiration for writing "Moving Stairs." Do you have a personal trait (strength or weakness) that you might like to incorporate into a fictional narrative? Describe the trait and the way you might like to explore it through story writing.
9. How does the author give readers strong messages about reading and writing in "Plague your Eyes," "Sympathy Pains," and "Choose Your Own Misadventure"?

Summarize the messages in two or three sentences. Do you think these are important messages for young people growing up today? Why or why not?

10. The final story of the collection ends with the sentence "As for the kitchen phone—the line went dead." What was your first thought when you finished reading this story? Why do you think David Lubar chose to make this the last story in the collection? Explain your answer.

ABOUT THE AUTHOR

David Lubar grew up in Morristown, New Jersey. His books include *Hidden Talents*, an ALA Best Book for Young Adults; *True Talents; Flip*, a VOYA Best Science Fiction, Fantasy, and Horror selection; the Weenies short-story collections *Attack of the Vampire Weenies, The Battle of the Red Hot Pepper Weenies, Beware the Ninja Weenies, The Curse of the Campfire Weenies, In the Land of the Lawn Weenies, Invasion of the Road Weenies,* and *Wipeout of the Wireless Weenies,* and the Nathan Abercrombie, Accidental Zombie series. He lives in Nazareth, Pennsylvania. You can visit him on the Web at www.davidlubar.com.